WINGSPAN

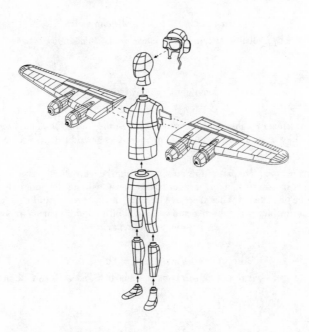

JEREMY HUGHES

Cillian Press |

First published in Great Britain in 2013
by Cillian Press Limited. 83 Ducie Street, Manchester M1 2JQ
www.cillianpress.co.uk

British Library Cataloguing in Publication Data.
A catalogue record for this book is available from the British Library.

Paperback ISBN: 978-0-9573155-8-7
eBook ISBN: 978-0-9573155-9-4

Cover Design: Roshana Rubin-Mayhew

Published by
Cillian Press – Manchester - 2013
www.cillianpress.co.uk

for
Renée,
Ursula & Theodore

The sun hath twice brought forth his tender green,
Twice clad the earth in lively lustiness.

Henry Howard, Earl of Surrey

PROLOGUE

Breconshire Constabulary

"C" Division
Police Station,
CRICKHOWELL.
17th September 1943.

Superintendent R. Jones,
County Police Office,
BRECON.

Sir,

I respectfully beg to report that at 10.30pm on 16th September, 1943, I received information from Glyn Williams, of Nant Farm, that an aeroplane had crashed on his land. Accompanied by P.C. 282, Arthur John, I proceeded to Nant Farm.

I was informed by WILLIAMS that he had heard the crash and he went out to investigate.

Accompanied by P.C. 282, Arthur John, I went to the crash site with WILLIAMS.

The debris at the site suggested a very large aeroplane. "G*I* W***ING" could be made out on one large section and the number 24-9305 was clear on what I understood to be part of the fuselage. There were nine bodies. WILLIAMS informed me that he had seen ten bodies. We searched the surrounding area but found nothing. The neighbouring farms were informed of the facts.

I notified the appropriate authorities.

I communicated with the coroner David Llewellyn Esq. and informed him of the facts. He requested me to ask Dr. Thomas to attend. Dr. Richard Thomas stated that the cause of the deaths was consistent with catastrophe.

I notified David Huws, Esq., J.P.

Please see attached statements by P.C. 282, Arthur John, and Glyn Williams.

Notice of deaths has been forwarded to the Coroner, David Llewellyn, Esq.

> I am, Sir,
> Your obedient Servant,
> Robert Prichard
> Inspector.

GLYN WILLIAMS states as follows:-

I am Glyn Williams of Nant Farm, Llanbedr.

On the evening of 16th September 1943 I was in the yard when a very large aeroplane flew over. I saw a flash and heard a loud bang shortly after.

I did not know what type of aeroplane it was so I took my shotgun and two dogs to investigate. I found the wreckage of the aeroplane spread over a large area. The dogs quickly found ten dead men. The aeroplane was American.

I returned to the farm and telephoned the police station.

At 11.00pm Inspector Prichard and P.C. John arrived at the farm. I directed them to the crash site but did not accompany them because I did not wish to see those poor men again.

When Inspector Prichard and P.C. John returned they said that they had counted nine bodies. I conceded that I might have mis-counted because I had been drinking beer at the Dragon Public House earlier. I am still sure that I counted ten men.

Inspector Prichard and P.C. John asked me to return with them to the crash site to search for the other man. We found nine bodies and after a wide search we found nothing else. When we returned to the farm Inspector Prichard requested that I inform my neighbours of the facts.

SIGNED. Glyn Williams.

The above statement was taken down by me at 2.25pm on 17th September 1943, at Crickhowell Police Station and read over by Williams before he signed it, in the presence of Inspector R. Prichard.

SIGNED. Arthur John, P.C. 282.

"C" Division
Police Station,
CRICKHOWELL.
17th September 1943.

Sir,

I respectfully beg to present this statement as being a true account of the events of the evening of 16th September 1943.

I was the duty constable at Crickhowell Station. I received a telephone call at 9.00pm from Mr. Glyn Williams of Nant Farm informing me that an aeroplane had crashed on his property. WILLIAMS was in a state of agitation. I established that the aeroplane had crashed on the land not on the dwelling.

I called for Inspector Robert Prichard on the way to Nant Farm.

When we arrived at Nant Farm WILLIAMS declined to accompany us to the crash site. He said: "I do not want to see those poor men again." He directed us to the site.

Inspector Prichard and I found the scene. There were nine bodies. WILLIAMS had stated that he had seen ten bodies.

We returned to Nant Farm.

I know WILLIAMS from previous incidents. He is a patron of the Dragon Public House. I asked him if he had attended that evening. He informed us that he had. Inspector Prichard informed WILLIAMS that there were nine bodies, at which WILLIAMS became angry and stated again that he had seen ten bodies.

Inspector Prichard said it was imperative to establish the facts and we had to return to the site. He was concerned that a man could be injured.

We returned to the site with WILLIAMS and his two dogs. We counted nine bodies. We searched the surrounding area for two hours but did not find another person.

WILLIAMS is certain he saw ten bodies.

WILLIAMS was instructed to inform his neighbours of the facts.

This being a true account of the events, by me, Sir,

Your obedient Servant,
Arthur John
P.C. 282

Chapter One

Death is afraid of me.

I have known this since my first flight. I had watched a pair of flyers at Bower's Field and it looked easy. The pilots waved and smiled and whooped and skirled around the sky. I could do that without an aeroplane, all on my lonesome.

I was swimming at Tullock's Steps with Marty Greenberg when I looked up at the bridge and said I could fly.

"No way Ho-zay," he said.

"It's easy. Those guys at Bower's were having a blast."

"But you've never been in one of those things."

"I don't need one. *I* can fly."

"Like to see that," he nodded.

"Watch me." I took the track up to the bridge and Marty was calling, *What you doing? Where you going?* I appeared on the bridge and made my way to the centre of the span. The trees either side of the valley reflected on the water moving slowly between the pillars.

Marty shaded his eyes and shouted: "Don't do nothin' stupid!"

I sat on the rail with my legs dangling, looking at my feet then focusing on the water between them. It looked deep and clear.

Marty's voice lassoed past me: "You're mad."

I stood on the rail, like a beam in the school gym. *You can come down now!* The rail was smooth and wide under the balls of my feet. I closed my eyes and took in the concoction of the trees' spring breaths, the rowan, the larch, the beech. I had been in their branches and now they were here to support me.

"What you doing?"

I opened my eyes. I wasn't looking down now. Marty's voice was spinning in the air with the birds' calls and the shushing breeze. I held out my arms in front of me as if I was about to dive, then took off.

That instant when my feet left the rail has for ever been me, held in the trees' breath, an airborne crucifixion preserved in my camera, veins and muscles the struts supporting my wings in the perfect aspect of flight, the dust between my toes like the dirt in the treads of undercarriage wheels.

"I thought you were dead, man," Marty said, when he came to visit me at home. "You were one stupid son-of-a-."

His face was sparking with the excitement of my flight. One son-of-a-. His eyes were the widest I'd ever seen them, then hooded by his brow the next, as a body involuntarily trying to interpret what it had witnessed, confused by the excitement and terror. But his mouth didn't change, fixed in a grin.

"This is to remind you *what* flies."

I unwrapped a model aeroplane.

We laughed.

"Not sure your mom's gonna like it."

There was an astonishing suspension of time. I was crucified on the belief of flight. My wings were frozen by the shutter speed of memory, a camera which spins 360° around me so that in this one I'm head on, the bridge's structure behind me, a skeleton with its feet on the river bed and its arms reaching to touch each side of the valley, its hands up to its wrists in leaves. This one has me in profile, the tips of my fingers in focus and the rest of me furring into a blur like mould. This one looking down on me, my hair parted by the whims of the water as it had slipped by me as I swam. Now it was the air which fingered my ribs rather than the currents which moved between the flat slabs of rock from which we dived and where we spread our towels, the hairs standing off our legs as we cooled. All in colour: red shorts, black hair, green eyes.

The model was the same as the planes we'd seen at Bower's Field. A Stearman, bright blue and yellow, its cockpit open to the elements, the pilots all teeth and leather so that I thought of them as flying sharks. They were so close and daring. They reeked too. They pushed through the crowd with their leather helmets cupped in their hands for the quarters and dimes, their faces grimed with the engine's exhausts, their eyes circles of white where their goggles had been. I wanted to be one.

The infinitesimal suspension was broken by the inexorable pull of gravity and the flight that followed lasted only seconds more, each a book of sensory experience. I was aware of my weight for the first time, not the pounds and ounces, but my *presence*. Here I was, a boy, flying off Tullock's Bridge while my friend Marty shielded his eyes from the sun, his left hand like the peak of a cap. It was a moment he would remember for the rest of his short life.

"I thought you were dead," he said. "I didn't think you'd do it. I can't believe you *did* do it."

I was looking at the model's wings.

"Why'd you do it?"

"Cos I thought I could, I guess."

"I guess."

I nodded and raised my eyebrows.

"Well, don't jump off anything again."

"I didn't jump. I flew."

Marty gripped his knees with his hands. "I'd better hit the road," he said. He stood up and I caught him in silhouette against the window and knew that Death would take him soon.

The first second consisted of the surprise and joy of being borne and born. I was peeled out of the constraints of my former being, a boy who had stepped off the bridge of innocence into the air of experience. Two was spent as a swallow, my legs straight out behind me and slightly apart like a forked tail aware of the air currents that bunched the flies this way and

11

that around the bridge's pillars. Three prepared me for the water and the fish I saw holding its position in the current, and the suddenness of the world beneath it.

"I kept looking at the spot where you went in and there was nothing," Marty said. "You crumpled into the water and disappeared. You were gone."

I thought of what he must have seen, the swirls and smashed surface repairing themselves to their former appearance, that smooth gliding which hinted of depth and mystery.

"Then you surfaced quietly and gently a few yards away, as if being held up."

I opened my eyes to a perfect flat sky. Within the water was another world. The quality of sky was such that it looked as if I could enter and disappear. A noise then, like trees in a breeze, and then I was touched.

"You're with us."

I moved my eyes to a nurse in the crisp leaf of her uniform.

Marty was always there but I can't remember the first time we met. That was lost in the beginnings of childhood. He witnessed my first flight, my first kiss and, I think, the first time a girl pumped my seed at the back of the Church of the Holy Shmoly.

Death singled him out for his beauty and his apparent lack of that self knowledge. Wherever we were together girls looked at him and their jaws dropped. If I hadn't seen it I wouldn't have believed it possible. But after a while they'd be saying to me, *That Marty guy's weird.*

He wasn't weird. He was just a beautiful innocent who would never see the plains of adulthood, a boy whose seed would never go beyond his own hand. A boy who would be killed by a girl who hadn't even got as far as deciding that he was 'weird'.

"They think you're it, Marty."

"I ain't no *it*. Stop saying so."

Any boy would have given up one of his balls for whatever it was that Marty had but he didn't want it. Perhaps that was another reason why Death took him.

I heard the instructors talking about me:

"That kid's scraping the tests."

"That's as maybe, but I'm telling you, he's the best damn flyer I've ever gone up with."

"That right?"

"I show him one thing, one little thing, and I never have to show him again. He just goes and slots it in somewhere. I tell you, he can out-fly the machine."

"But the rest?"

"Shoot the rest, it's kids who can fly the damn planes we need. This kid would fly to the moon and back if I let him."

After Tullock's Bridge, I didn't need instruction. I knew how the plane would react before it happened, whether it was wind or rain or sleet or sun or engine failure or bullets or missiles or just plain turbulence. It was nothing to me. I'd learned everything in my descent to the river's level drifting breadth, and I'd done it while listening to the leaves' soft applause as I did so.

Sitting behind me in the trainer the instructor would say, "You sure you've not done this before?"

I wanted to say, *Just strap an engine to my back and a bomb to my belly and let me go.*

The magneto quit and the instructor took over but was struggling to take control. There was no power, we couldn't climb, the magneto wouldn't respond and the trees below looked like concrete.

"She's mine, Sir," I said. I slapped the rudder and set her down hot.

"Son-of-a-bitch!" my instructor hollered at me as he got down from the plane. "You make me sick. You're a God-damn bitch, no doubt about it." He marched me straight to another ship. "Now take this piece of shit and show me you can fly."

That's how I went solo. No nerves, just a feeling that this was what I was for. I didn't need to think about anything, checking this and that. It was there in my make up. It's what I was. I made that baby dance.

"If I ever see you do that again, I'll ground you," the instructor said when

I landed, "but it sure was beautiful." I moved closer to the big beautiful gals.

They don't know what I know. If they don't wash out on the way they all want to be aces, flying solo forever in Mustangs, Thunderbolts and Warhawks. But that's not what it's all about. They're thinking of the glory of flying. They don't know it's about being at one with the machine. It's nothing to do with them as individuals, it's the need for fighter pilots or transport pilots or bomber pilots. They're just another part of the machine, and I want to be in the most beautiful baby ever to fly. The B17. I want to be that indescribable something doctors try to find to determine whether you're alive or dead, what priests talk about so freely without actually being able to define it. I am the aeroplane's brain. I am its soul. Why would anyone want to fly with one engine when you can fly with four? It's like having an orchestra at your disposal, conducting them in your very own *Flight of the Humble B*! That's it. The fighters buzz around like insects but we'll just swat them away. Oh boy.

A lot of these guys are dying before they can even get into the war. They just can't do the flying. They get airsick or they can't work out which way's up. Some think they're bona fide aces already until the instructor tells them they're not going to kill them today, thank you, nor have the opportunity to kill anyone else, let alone slam one of Uncle Sam's shiny machines into the ground. Some of them will still get to fly, though, in a bomber crew.

I was always the tallest kid in the class and when I realised I could fly I started to see myself as an albatross, spending all day on outspread wings without so much as a flap. Then I thought of myself as a buzzard, but a carrion feeder wasn't right for a would-be pilot. Then it was an eagle, a golden bird, something that had the ability to attack and defend, single out its prey from a great distance. That was me, dangerously beautiful. Six feet four and a half inches, one hundred and ninety six pounds. My arms outstretched are six feet eight and a half inches. I've *always* been a bomber.

I wasn't that big when Marty got me out of the river, but on the way.

Marty wasn't small either, and a tough cookie, though he would never think of himself as such. As quiet and gentle as anyone I've known but no push over. I should have been protecting him but it was the other way round, like when we were out of the neighbourhood and came across some guys who thought it would be fun to ride us. People my size often get singled out for special attention, as if the world isn't for us when some guy wants to prove himself somehow, usually a little guy who, for whatever reason, decides that today you're gonna be the way he makes himself feel better about whatever it is in his core which makes him feel inadequate.

So these guys are cool, you know, all slick moves and talk a talk Marty and I think strange. I see them first on the other side of the street, spot them a whole day and several miles before they see us, and when they do I know they'll be over, slapping each other and nodding and sure enough, they cross. I wonder what's coming exactly, but know it's not going to be hello. It's one of those scenes in a Chaplin film: two people approach each other on the sidewalk and try to avoid each other but both go the same way. You go this way, they go that way too. Laughter. But this isn't funny.

I am polite. "Excuse me," I say.

"Excuse me?" he says.

"Yes." I stand to one side. Marty's looking at us both. The guy's buddies are all ants in their pants.

He's more or less on my toes now, looking up into my face. "Excuse me? What kinda talk's *that*? Ex*cuse* me? You sound like a *girl*. You a *girl*?"

He pulls a knife and its blade flicks out as clean as a snake's tongue. Marty catches the guy's wrist with his left hand and punches him straight in the face with his right in one movement and the guy hits the deck. "Which one of you's next?" he says, as if he's trying to help them decide.

They back off without picking up their buddy. Marty drops the knife down a storm drain and huffs, "*How* unfriendly can you get?"

Not really meant for this world.

I never told anyone about the other side, not that anyone ever asked me. In fact, no one ever asked me about the flight at all, apart from why I did it. People were pussy-footing about, asking was I unhappy, did I want to die, was there a girl? No. No. No. I had an epiphany but I couldn't put it like that. I told them what would get me out of the hole: I wanted to do something exciting.

They lectured me about how I'd put a lot of people to a lot of trouble for my stupid prank. It was all drowned out by the leaves' applause, the music the other side, and the long silence when my muscles and bones worked with each other to enable me to fly again.

Chapter Two

I suppose it was unreasonable to have wanted both of my parents at my fiftieth birthday. How many people *do* for the occasion? But it wouldn't have been possible anyway, never having known my father other than as a two dimensional black and white photograph on the mantelpiece throughout my childhood, and my mother falling short by a few months. It would only have hurt her in all probability, being reminded of the fifty long years that had passed since the man whom she loved had met his maker in 1943. That was a good way of putting it. The day she received the news that he would not be coming back, she shook off her faith like an ill-fitting coat. Oh she tried, she said, to see it all as part of God's greater plan, that it was merely a minuscule event in the world's great tragedy. But she couldn't sustain it. She had devoted herself to church, attending St. Michael's ever since she could remember: Sunday school, bible class, summer fêtes, harvest festivals, lent. The lot. Then she stopped going, just like that.

"There is no such thing as Christ or God," she said when I came home from school one day talking about raising the dead, feeding the five thousand, making the blind see. "That's all baloney." That was one of Dad's words, not a Suffolk word. Dad, as it happens, is a word I've never used. "That's your father," Mum would say, showing me photographs of him. She never referred to him as Dad, either. I suppose I would have called him Dad if I'd known him. He was always 'my father', as if he was some distance away and would return, when in fact he would never come back. Mum could have been at my birthday, I'm sure, but fifty years is a long time to be on your own and I understand she wanted to go. She had been

17

there for my twenty-first and thirtieth and fortieth, so she'd done her bit.

We are here today to celebrate Gail's life, a life lived in the midst of evil, a life that conjoined in love and produced new life. A great life, because life itself is great.

Although I didn't know her, it is clear to me from the conversations I have had that Gail was a kind and loving person, a person who loved the people close to her, a person always willing to help those in need. I think it is possible to see those qualities in the photographs we have here.

She was born in Suffolk in February 1923 just after the Great War. She was lonely as a child and planned to have lots of children when the time came. That time was 1942, when she met the man with whom she wanted to live for the rest of her life.

Gail met Grayson – Gray – when the world was fighting the evil that threatened it. It was frightening and exciting, young men and women living for the moment. They met at the base and I think of them dancing to a big band. For Gail it was love at first sight.

That's exactly what she said. She told me so many times about how she met my father that I sometimes believed I must have been there. There was a glitterball, she said, in the hangar where they were dancing, and ribbons and taffeta dresses and men in uniforms and ties with small tight knots. She said that when dad held her close he felt ironed and strong. He was twenty-one and she was twenty. "He was dashing." She actually said dashing. "He was like a film star, neat and clean and handsome. And he had such a wonderful voice. Nothing like the boys I was used to. He said it was nothing special in America. I couldn't tell. I felt as if I was in a film. It was unbelievable. I should have known it was fantasy but I couldn't help myself." She saw the aeroplanes every day but never thought she would dance with one of the pilots. Or marry him. "A man of twenty-one responsible for those great big machines and nine other men. They were all just boys."

When I look at the photographs out here I wonder what they said to each other, what they found in each other. Thousands of miles from home he fell in love with a girl from a small English village. Their love produced a boy who became a special man, special because he has shaped the lives of many boys and girls.

I am special?

You are half of your mother and half of your father, he says, addressing me now. *You might think she lived with a broken heart but you must realise that you are the embodiment of your parents and therefore the embodiment of the love that made you, a reminder every day of how extraordinary and wonderful love is. He who believes in Christ shall have everlasting life. Your father gave his life for Gail, and for all of us gathered here today.*

I wonder what mum would make of all this. It's turning into a lecture on the war. I suppose it's to be expected, considering. We felt it daily. Everyone had a story in the villages near the base. *Over sexed, over paid and over here* doesn't fit the photograph of my father placed next to one of Mum at the front, the photograph on the mantelpiece throughout my childhood. He was the sadness Mum wore like a heavy piece of jewellery, though she never wore any, apart from the wedding ring. I have it now. It's tiny. She never took it off even when she had her tonsils excised.

And this is where I must talk about Gail's broken heart. Gray was killed in action in 1943 and I am told she never recovered. They had such little time together.

No time.

Love is the greatest capacity that God bestows upon us. To be separated from those we love is a terrible burden to bear. It is entirely apt to remember these words from Romans: "I am convinced that neither death, nor life, nor angels, nor rulers, nor things present, nor things to come, nor powers, nor height, nor depth, nor anything else in all creation, will be able to separate us from the love of God in Christ Jesus our Lord."

I am trying not to cry now. I didn't expect to and won't let myself. "If there was a God he wouldn't have allowed this to happen to anyone," Mum said. "No one should have to go through this." She meant losing my father. I concentrate on the minister's white robe and the sky-blue sash draped around his neck. And suddenly I am transported into that recurring childhood dream in which I sat in my father's plane with my hand on top of his as he moved the controls between us.

"God so loved the world that he gave His only Son, so that everyone who believes in him may not perish but may have eternal life." So it is with Gail and Gray, who loved each other. It is important that we remember that in God there are no broken hearts. Gail will be with Gray now, as one day we shall all be together.

But now she is gone.

She took pride in going to secretarial school, learning touch-typing on huge manual typewriters before the advent of the more finger-friendly electric machines. She was good at her job, took great pride in her efficiency.

"We wouldn't have won the war being sloppy," she'd said to me.

When she retired she didn't know what to do with herself. She advertised her services in the local paper and the post office window and was always busy with something.

When I was at an age at which my curiosity caused me to enquire about my father, she told me there was nothing to know other than what she'd already told me. "I met him, loved him, married him, lost him. That's all there is."

"But where was he from? What did he do before the war? What about his family in the States?"

"All that matters is what I've told you."

It was just Mum and me the whole time. There were no other men. No one could possibly have matched the film-set presence of my father. We were in a village where it was considered pretentious if you *didn't* drop your aitches.

This is all such a charade. What the minister doesn't say is that she never wore trousers and never went in a pub. Public House, she said. She used words like 'bloody' and 'bugger' and 'sod' when she was very angry and would explode after long festering silences. And instead of rebelling against her parental constrictions, I just went along with them. I'd look at my father's photograph on the mantelpiece and immediately feel her emptiness. His absence pervaded every room in the house. For Mum, he was every breath in and every breath out. Occasionally I found her holding his photograph against her breast, or talking to him. On my tenth birthday I heard her crying in her room.

In the midst of life we are in death.

In many ways I had never grown up because Mum 'protected' me from the world. I *did* have girlfriends but they never lasted. A different man would have left but I couldn't. Just couldn't. She had this gaping hole in her which I went some way to filling. One girl, Sylvia, spat, "I don't want to marry your mother!" when she walked away.

I didn't have a clue what to do about the funeral and was glad when the undertaker took over and I was able to let him get on with it. People my age assess their position, their status, the wife, the kids at university, the house, the grounds, the second home, the retirement within reach. As a headteacher (Mum preferred '-master') I have achieved only the respect of those working alongside or beneath me. It's been easy. As a teacher I was uninspiring but as it counts for nothing when climbing the managerial ladder, it was no hindrance. I completed all administration meticulously and way before deadline, carried out everything managers delegated. I got every promotion I applied for, trod on nobody's toes and was inoffensive to the point of being bland. And in interviews I didn't have to pretend to be anything other than what I was. I could have been a Head years before I was but I was restricted to a daily travelling distance from Mum. "This is your home. What do you want another house for?"

I walked into the crematorium behind Mum's coffin as the undertaker directed and I was surprised to see so many people there. Neighbours. She was a good neighbour. "You must help one another or nothing will be achieved." There were also people I didn't recognise representing parts of her life I had only heard about.

May God in his infinite love and mercy
bring the whole Church,
living and departed in the Lord Jesus,
to a joyful resurrection
and the fulfilment of his eternal kingdom.

The undertaker stood me at the door while people walked past me and shook my hand. Then the undertaker suggested I stand by the flowers outside. There was my tribute, a blooming typewriter. It could have represented me too.

Many people said, *If there's anything I can do.* And one man gave me his card. "Your mother did some work for me. I wanted to pay my respects."

I expect there were many wedding photographs similar to my parents' on mantelpieces in villages around American bases. My father was so smart. He stands with such grace and authority at St. Michael's and makes it look easy. He was twenty-one! When I look at myself in the full-length mirror in Mum's room I see a tame and acquired absence. When I smile I do not light up the room as my father's smile lights up his photographs. It's only then that I realise that Mum must have been a 'looker'. My father is obviously handsome and when I've considered the wedding photograph I have always been drawn to him. After all, I *knew* Mum. She has that white-faced English prettiness you see in films of the period.

But Mum was gone now and I was alone. No position for a man, or anyone for that matter, on the cusp of their fiftieth. As I left the crematorium I slipped a copy of the Funeral Service in my suit pocket and felt rather pleased that she was dead.

The first thing I bought after Mum died was a model of a Flying Fortress. I remember holding a large model box in my arms as a small boy in Woollies in Norwich and Mum taking it off me: "Now come on, you don't want to waste your pocket money on that kind of thing," she said, putting it back on the shelf.

There was no one to say no now, as the words Flying Fortress seemed to jut out in three dimensions from the other kits on the shelf: Lancaster, Wellington, Short Stirling, Superfortress.

"I've not made one of these before," I said to the man who served me.

"You mean that particular kit or at all?"

"At all," I said, a little self-consciously.

"Right. You'll need some glue and paints. You gonna paint it?"

"I suppose so."

"It's only a bit of plastic if you don't," he said. "Good. Right. Let's see." He took the box from me and read from it. "One of these, one of these…" as he took the small pots of paint from the stand. "You'll need a few brushes as well, and some thinners. You've never made one, right?"

"That's right."

"Ok. You'll need a craft knife, sandpaper to smooth rough edges – there's always rough edges when you take the pieces off the sprues – and a couple of small cramps. Oh yeah, and some tape. It's good to have a space where you can leave it and go back to it, too. Get yourself a magazine. They're full of tips." He handed me the carrier bag with the name of the shop on it, the weight of the plastic kit now more significant with the rest of the paraphernalia necessary to build it.

I was about six years old when they started. I would close my eyes and rub my feet together under the blankets, then find myself standing at the top of the stairs. I'd put my arms out in front of me and let myself fall, and as I did so, some extraordinary force would take me in its arms until I was in the horizontal. And as I felt myself supported I spread my arms out like wings. My back brushed against the ceiling as I looked down on the patterned carpet's fields. I went round and round the light. Then I saw myself in the mirror Mother always checked herself in before she faced the world, and the bookcase with my set of Encyclopaedia Britannica. Once I'd seen all was in order, I'd return to the landing just as gently as I'd taken off. That feeling was profound. I was light and strong and special.

But at that moment when I rubbed my feet under the blanket I didn't know that I *would* dream about flying. Sometimes the dream that followed was different. I would find myself at the entrance of a cave which I had to enter and at some point I would encounter the monster. I *knew* I would but it was always a shock when it appeared, filling the space with its bulk. Physically it was a huge, violent scribble of pencil, the strokes making up its black fur and huge clawed paws, its eyes white patches where the pencil had been erased. It terrified me, but I would wake up then sleep with no further trouble. The dreams about flying with my father started later.

Taking the box out of the large paper bag sent a tingle through me. The illustration was the kind that got me all excited in Woollies when I was a child. I had longed to make one and it was sad *how* long. The aircraft was in the thick of action, its guns blazing at the German fighters plaguing it. It was a Christmas moment when I took off the lid and saw the olive green pieces and the plane's glazed parts on a separate frame. I slit the bags to examine the fuselage, wings, wheels, propellers, seats. Finding the latter, I looked for the pilots. I wanted to have my father in my hand. But there was no pilot. I looked at the instructions: the kit didn't come with a crew of any kind. Considering that it could be made with its undercarriage up for flight, it seemed odd that there was no crew to fly it. This was the Marie Celeste of the skies.

The cockpit was first in the instruction booklet, with numbered 'flags' to indicate the colour each piece was to be painted. Hell, that didn't matter to me. I was making a model to be closer to the father I'd never known. It didn't matter what colour the seats and straps had to be, I wanted him *there* in the hot seat. The inside didn't matter. Just having the aeroplane made up and on display somewhere in the house would create his presence for me, albeit a tenuous and vicarious one.

I heard two mothers talking about me at the school summer fayre. I was checking the pegs outside the marquee which we'd put up for the PTA to shelter from the sun or rain, whichever the English weather had planned, when I heard them:

"What's up with *him*, you think?"

"Up?"

"You know, where's his wife?"

"Not married."

"Partner then."

"He lives with his mother, apparently."

"He's gay, I knew it."

"No, no. There *was* a woman, once, I believe."

"That's just a front. They often do that."

"'They'?"

"Gay men. They're often great professionally and cover their tracks."

"There are no tracks to cover, are there? He's just a man who lives with his mother."

"Mmm. Well, it's not right. You must admit, it's a *little* strange."

"I suppose."

"He'd be taken more seriously if he *was* married and had kids."

"We haven't got any complaints. He's so professional."

The exchange stopped and I gave it a few moments before entering the marquee. "Good afternoon, ladies!" I said. "My, you're both looking very summery." As I walked out I heard, "Definitely gay."

My fiftieth birthday dinner was simple and private. I set up the table for three. I put my father's photograph on one placemat and a photograph of my mother on another. Three glasses. I filled mine and clinked theirs. Cheers.

Rabbit. I opened a tin of rice pudding for dessert, my favourite. I placed a tea- light on top of the chocolate sponge I'd bought from the baker's and put it on the table between Mum and Dad. Their faces glowed.

I get it now, my schoolboy pals' obsession for Airfix models. They fill a need within each little boy, put them at the controls of an exciting aeroplane or terrifying tank. That was all my pals seemed to make. Ships hardly got made, their enormous presence beyond the realms of plastic bits in a flimsy cardboard box. But an aeroplane was something else. You can put yourself in that seat and look out over the nose or along the wings, or behind one of the guns and squint down the barrel to catch an enemy fighter in the sights as its wing guns spit lead at you.

I realised then that I didn't have an Airfix kit, but Revell. Did it matter? I just wanted a model of what my father had commanded. I went back to the shop.

"I was wondering – and I know this might sound odd – but there are no pilots in the kit, no crew at all."

"Really? I didn't know that."

"Can't fly a plane without a crew!

"You're right there."

"I just wondered, do the Airfix models come with pilots?"

"I think so. Let's have a look." He opened the box of a nearby kit. "This one does so I expect they all do."

"Do Airfix have a Flying Fortress?"

"We haven't got one but I can get one in for you."

"Ok. I suppose I'd better finish the one I've got, first. Maybe later."

I didn't leave the shop immediately. When I bought the Fortress I'd been business-like, walked in, got what I wanted and left. Now I look around, though 'around' is odd for a shop so small. The models are stacked deeply on the shelves and I pull them out of the boxes to examine the illustrations I loved as a boy: they haven't changed. There are tanks and armoured cars, ships and soldiers. It's the aeroplanes which fascinate me, though – the big bombers. "If you're interested in the Fortress, you might like these," the proprietor said. He went to the small boxes and pulled out a couple. "These fought alongside them, escorted them."

He held a Mustang in one hand and a Thunderbolt in the other. I took the Mustang from him. The illustration showed a dynamic machine fiercer than the elegance of a Spitfire. Then I took the Thunderbolt, stubbier and more compact, more bulldog-like. "I'll take this one."

But I needed to complete the Fortress, so I got straight into it. I wanted it whole in my hands. Just give me the frames and numbered boxes and glue and I'm off. The assembly instructions are so clear and simple. If only life could be like this, numbered parts and arrows to show you where to put them. A drop of glue and there you go.

Some of the small parts are a devil to hold and glue and fix in place. I smear the glue and it's messy. I get the tweezers, with which I pull out my nostril hair, from the bathroom cabinet. To begin with they help, but I still haven't the dexterity to position things without messing the glue.

I open the door to a man I recognise from somewhere.

"Your mother did some work for me. I was at the funeral?"

"I remember."

"She – your mother, I mean Gail – gave me something to look after for her. I didn't think the funeral was the right time to mention it. Perhaps you could fetch it now."

"What is it?"

"I've had it years. It's a box."

"Box."

"Yes, couldn't have it in the house, she said."

"What's in it?"

"I've no idea. I never asked."

"You've not looked?"

"Heavens no. Besides, it's locked. Been in my barn for years."

"My mother did some work for you, you say?"

"George Chapman," he said, offering his hand. "She gave me this box years ago, said she'd have it back one day and would I look after it. She never did, ask for it back I mean, so I thought you'd better have it now."

"Well, yes, if it's something that belonged to my mother."

"That's right, it belongs to you."

"Yes it does, I suppose." Then I remembered myself: "I'm sorry, how rude of me. Would you like a cup of tea?"

We stepped into the house. George stood in the hallway next to the bookcase and I ushered him into the kitchen.

"Actually, I'd prefer coffee."

"It'll have to be instant."

"I didn't expect anything else. Oh, now who's being rude!"

We shared a smile and the awkwardness between us began to dissipate. He was smart, a similar age to my mother, with his dense grey hair combed back and a ruddy complexion I associated with years and years of shaving every morning. His hands were brown around the mug of coffee.

"She was a very good woman, your mother. Meticulous in everything she did for me, not like the young ones these days. Can't write their name let alone anyone else's. But you know all about that, being a teacher."

"I'm a Head, so don't get to see much pupils' work."

"Anyway, your mother was the best."

"She certainly drilled it into me, the importance of getting things just so."

27

"She talked about you. She was very proud." He appeared to remember something. "You'll need your car."

"I'm sorry?"

"For the box."

I take the model shop owner's advice and get myself a magazine. It makes me feel strangely inadequate. Tips be damned. In an attempt for authenticity modellers track down all sorts of information about the aircraft, the squadrons and the pilots. They even represent exhaust smuts on the fuselage or bullet holes or battle damage. All I want is to try and understand my father, somehow, know a little about what he did when he was alive. I just want to get the thing done and don't care whether the pieces fit exactly.

When I walk through the village I feel a kind of lightness, as if I've lost weight. I realise, too, that I haven't cried. I have spent my whole life joined to Mum and now that she's gone I think there should have been a flood. It's not that I ever resented her, apart from the odd teenage moment. I think it's because I always felt for her. She was a simple girl who met a man from another world, fell in love and, as with many others during the war, lost. The village must have been a shock for my father, too. Hardly any cars, horses doing the heavy work on the land and a way of life that must have been medieval to him. For Mum, a gamekeeper's daughter in rural Suffolk, a pilot officer in uniform speaking like someone from a Hollywood film was practically god-like. He, too, would have found her just as strange, supplementing the limits of rationing with fare from the field, wood and hedge: rabbit, pigeon, pheasant.

She taught me how to prepare them all for the pot on the table which still stands four-square in the kitchen, made by my great grandfather, she said, so I've never been squeamish of blood and guts. That's life and death in the country. There was always something dead hanging in the outhouse.

To watch her prepare a rabbit was a treat on a Sunday. She didn't believe in a roast. "There's only two of us." My grandfather would have gutted it so all Mum had to do was skin it. She put a board on the table and set about the ritual with the knife and steel, the swift sounds of metal against metal like a mini sword fight in her hands. She *always* sharpened the knife before she used it. "It's got to be keen to make it clean." Razor sharp, it parted fur and skin with an ease which pleased her.

She ran the knife around the joint in each back leg, snapped it, cut the sinews, slit the skin on the inside and pushed the stump through. She pulled the pelt down the carcase in one slick movement, the sound of un-kissing, something I've never heard anywhere else, as if she were relieving a four-legged fruit of its skin. She repeated the procedure with the front legs, snicked through the neck, the head now hooded like an early photographer, looking at this last image of itself upside down.

I must have been eight years old when I started doing all this for myself. Mum would still sharpen the knife, however, and stood over me as I relieved the rabbit of its furry self, putting her hand on mine to show me exactly where to put it, where to introduce the knife's dog-snout point. In those days all the rabbits came from my grandfather. Now I usually get them from the butcher's where they hang outside the shop like empty puppets waiting for hands to animate them.

I can't be bothered with painting the cockpit before assembly. I'm not going to be looking at it that closely, especially as the pilot's missing. I quite like the guns, though, and the simplicity of the mechanism which allows the ball turret gun in the belly to swivel. When I get the wings on, the plane is huge. My schoolboy pals hung them from their bedroom ceilings.

Once it's completed I think that, actually, there's not that much to it. Now that I can see it whole and run through the process, it was straightforward.

Painting it is next. I have a couple of brushes and I set about the large areas. To do it properly, I should have painted all the parts before assembly, at least, that's what I've learned from the magazine. The engines, undercarriage, guns and cockpit glass are going to be a fiddle. I don't count on how long it's going to take, either. I tire and lose patience. In the end I don't care about the accuracy. The underside is meant to be grey and the topside camouflaged, and there's a line which should be straight where they meet. There is black on the wings' leading edges, too. A serious modeller would use tape and an airbrush to define such things but I just want to get it done. It's good enough. I bet the real things weren't painted that straight anyway.

The Thunderbolt's instructions indicate gluing the pilot to its seat. A spot of glue on his flat grey buttocks and I sit him on it. He's ready to fly. I look at him as closely as I can with my myopic eyes. The detail is surprisingly good. He's wearing a helmet, flying suit and boots. He sits with one leg slightly in front of the other and his hands are between his legs as if he's holding a joy-stick. I look more closely with a magnifying glass. *Dad, is that you?* One of the few things I do know about Fortresses is that they didn't have a stick, but a control column on which was mounted a kind of steering wheel, so this couldn't be my father. Still, it doesn't stop me from examining this little man.

It gives me pleasure to consider him like this. Now I imagine him flying, sparking around the sky like a vigilant bee defending its cumbersome queen as she struggles to carry her load, diving at anything which might prevent her from doing so. His nose is yellow, the tail is red: an exotic American species which is here to defend the queens releasing their loads every day. I take the metaphor as far as I can. On Earth, I think of the pilot scalping off his helmet and goggles, feeling that exhaustion which must have come from being cramped in the cockpit and throwing his plane about the sky, pressed into himself as he engaged the enemy, thinking as a fighter, manoeuvring to kill. His buttocks creased, his body clammy, his feet heavy and his legs and shoulders aching. That beer tastes good in the mess later. The bunk feels even better as he drifts into the clouds of sleep. There is no white silk scarf or *Tally-ho!* and in my hand he is not my father. He's a small grey plastic fighter pilot.

I am on the train back from a Friday meeting in London, feeling that odd uncleanliness I always feel after being there, and I look around me. Complexions blotchy after a week at work reflected in the carriage windows in which eyes recognise themselves, then look through to the lights of distant farms. The noise of college kids bringing them back to reality, the kids at home, the mortgage, the car payments, the ageing parents, the bewilderment of middle age on a middle income, and realising now, as never before, that this is what they had not imagined when they had to write that essay in school – *What I shall be doing when I am fifty* – *I'll be rich and famous, married to a handsome man/beautiful woman and have beautiful kids, drive a Rolls Royce and swim in my pool every day, go to America on holiday, buy all my food at Marks & Spencer's...*But here they are, tired, in a carriage of tired people whose essays are the same as theirs. 'Could have done better' written on their faces, surfacing from their graveyard to think of what keeps them on track, the family, the home, the mortgage for which they do this day in day out. The world which no one else on this train knows, that intimate gulf between their pinstripe or two-piece, and still the college kids are laughing at the end of the carriage, making arrangements for a wild weekend, putting off their essays. That's when I cry.

Chapter Three

2nd March 1942

Buzzing around in a Stearman is one thing, taking off in a four-engined Fort is another. The Stearman takes you into a different element; the Fortress takes you beyond it, close to whatever is on the other side. You look down on the world or slow-moving clouds drifting like floes of ice. Some days I break through and it is as if I am standing on Tullock's Bridge looking down the valley at the hills in the sun. Marty. Maybe he is up there somewhere.

It is quite something to be on the ground, look up at the sky and *know* that you have been the other side of those clouds and looked down on them. And looked up from the ship at the night's cosmic city. This is where I am comfortable, a never-place, and for short intense periods, bullets and flak try to knock me out of it.

Death is much closer here, too. Even if a ship explodes in mid-air, Death takes each man separately. It could be neat, a single bullet or piece of flak making a small hole in a body, or it could be messy, blasting a man into pieces that could never be put back together into a semblance of his former self.

Since Marty died in front of me and since I knew Death would never pin me down, I have witnessed many men die. There is nothing strange about that, but unlike me, these men always go up thinking they might not come back. When they don't, we paint their names on the walls. Jo Marinetti, Illinois; Cliff Zuckker, New York; Trent Crupps, Wisconsin. Then the replacements arrive wondering what these names are about, hoping *their* names will never be painted when they find out. "The names tell you all you need to know."

Guys do all sorts of stuff to keep Death at arms' length, wearing charms or keeping a routine which means certain death if they forget it or deviate from it in any way. There are even ships associated with luck. *The Flying Pig* was damaged and made it back so many times that the crew renamed her *Holey Cow*.

Death keeps on spitting its hot metals at me. It even tries to freeze me, blowing out the cockpit glass so that even the thick sheepskins feel like pyjamas rather than mattresses, which is how they feel at ground level. With the boots, flak jacket, oxygen mask, goggles, earphones and a parachute, you feel like a strange animal. You are so tired when you get back that your modest bunk is the most wonderful bed you've ever slept in.

The commander's seat is my niche, my place in the world. Looking out over the wings is looking along my arms: 103 feet 9 inches. Being the ship's commander, I take a jeep out to her. That's what I do when there is no one around. More than once I have slept inside her long belly: 74 feet 4 inches.

I walk around her. I think I must be regarded as a conscientious commander, nothing more, though I'm sure there may be crewmen who think I am a little crazy. They want to spend as little time inside her as possible and the sooner the tour is over, the better. Twenty-five missions. They would be lucky. I never worry about such things. My baby will always get me back even though a strong man could poke a screwdriver through her skin. She is, in reality, a crate of bombs and we merely deliver them. She has thirteen Browning .50 calibre machine guns poking out in all directions, even an electrohydraulic one swivelling under her, in which a little guy curls up like a mouse with the sights between his knees.

It is like stepping back in time. The villages. The churches. The pubs. I only had one pint of warm brown beer, though. I couldn't stand it. It was good to get that learned early because when I went to London I didn't want that awful feeling of carrying a heavy load around and having to empty my bladder frequently. It stopped me from enjoying myself. There are girls. Lots of girls. And good food, which is not what I expected, considering the rationing. If you have the money, which I do, which all we Americans do, you can get whatever you want. Before we went to London, the camp doc lectured us about VD and not putting it about, or being taken for suckers and getting more than we bargained for. We all knew the stories about guys who'd been lured somewhere and woken up with a light wallet and an unpleasant itch downstairs. Or beaten up. But that was never going to happen to me.

I didn't even need to wish to meet girls when I was with Marty. They just appeared, wherever we were. We'd been fishing downstream from Tullock's Bridge, the day he died. The large flat slabs of stone where we lay out in the sun were also perfect places on which to sit and dangle our feet in the water and cast into the deep runs. We had half a dozen trout between us, which came sparkling to us through the clear water, their flanks' bright stars dulling as their lives escaped them on the stone. I couldn't think of it as Death being present, actually *taking* their lives.

Something similar happened to Marty. I saw his pupils dilate and they stayed like that. It was as if that's from where his life escaped. His pupils did not open to gather light, they let something out. This is what people everywhere were afraid of but it was utterly serene. Seeing men die wouldn't always be like that.

1. Fire Guard and call clear – LEFT Right
2. Fire Switch – ON
3. Battery switches and inverters – ON & CHECKED
4. Parking Brakes – Hydraulic Check – ON & CHECKED
5. Booster Pumps – Pressure – ON & CHECKED
6. Carburettor Filters – Open
7. Fuel Quantity – Gallons per tank
8. Start Engines: both magnetos on after one revolution
9. Flight Indicator & Vacuum Pressures – CHECKED
10. Radio – On
11. Check Instruments – CHECKED

12. Crew Report

13. Radio Call & Altimeter – SET

I start looking at guys and try to spot which ones are going to get it. Maybe it's the 'good' ones first. Maybe it's those with a gang of siblings who can 'afford' to be lost. Maybe it's those with wives and kids at home who have plenty to mourn them. The only thing that makes sense is that it's entirely random. And it isn't necessarily in combat. Put a bunch of young guys in a mix with high explosives, deadly weapons and complex machines and you're going to have problems, even on the ground. There's bound to be human error however much men are trained. There's no accounting for accidents. Death is happy to take take take. Anyhow. Anywhere. Any time.

I don't ever expect to be in London again. The plan – *the plan* – was to finish the war and go home and London would be something to remember. I didn't want to waste it. I stood at the top of the steps at the National Gallery looking over Trafalgar Square. Whilst I was throttling a bomber over France and Germany under attack from fighters and flak, people here were feeding pigeons. You could stand here with your arms out and they'd be on you almost immediately. You were a target on which to swoop and cover in crap. Boom! The stray cats of the bird world. Or something like that.

It was while I was watching this that I was bumped. As I turned to face the person who had bumped me, I caught something else in my peripheral vision. It must have been my pilot's sense, my cockpit vision. The person who bumped me was a woman, the person in my peripheral vision another, whose wrist I grabbed and lifted. I took in the wallet in her hand first, then her look of horror at being caught. "Thank you," I said, as I took my wallet from her hand. They shot looks at each other, then ran. "That's not very friendly!" I called after them. I wasn't angry, but felt sorry for them. "Hey, come back!" I held out my hand like a gun and sighted them in front of my thumb. The wallet snatcher had good legs.

I spent a few hours in the gallery. A man had set up an easel in front of a painting and was copying it. I walked through the galleries and ended up at the same spot, so sat on a bench nearby and watched him. I hadn't thought about mixing colours since I was a boy. Red and yellow make orange. Blue and yellow make green. He worked on hues in the sky. I wanted to tell him that the sky isn't blue, that some days it's flying through metal. People feeding pigeons. A man copying a painting. Men flying and dying.

The Lyceum was busy when I arrived. A band played on a stage and the floor was spinning with GIs and girls. Colourful. Blue and red make purple. I realised I'd missed this. It seemed my mood was similar to the colour of my uniform, to the colours of my daily experience. Here there were girls in primary and secondary and tertiary colours, all just fine to look at. I recognised the wallet snatcher from her legs first. She was talking to a GI and her pal was behind him. The pal clocked me and walked away quickly. The wallet snatcher turned and her face stiffened. I smiled, "Hello, how lovely to see you again." Hell, she looked uncomfortable! A looker though. I wondered about the colour mix of her eyes. Her lips were primary. Her dress, the colour of a sky I once saw as I broke through the overcast at twelve thousand feet.

She looked past me, nervous.

"Don't worry, I'm not going to cause you any trouble. Shall we have a drink?"

"I have to catch up with my friend."

"I don't think you need to worry about her. Come on. No tricks."

I held out my hand and she took it, her face relaxing. "Do you mind if I just pop to the cloakroom?"

"Sure, go ahead."

She gave me the glass she had in her other hand, and smiled, eyes fixed in mine. I admired her as she walked around the edge of the dance floor to the cloakroom. It was fifteen minutes before I realised she wasn't coming back.

1. Brakes – Locked
2. Trim Tabs – SET
3. Exercise Turbos and Props

4. Check Generators – CHECKED & OFF
5. Run up Engines

I hadn't even had the chance to dance with her. I held her small wrist to retrieve my wallet, held her hand as she smiled at me. That touch coursed through me slowly like bourbon or whiskey. By the time I realised she wasn't coming back it had reached a point over my shoulders. By the time I got back to my hotel, it was in my bones. Her legs! Hell! I wanted to feel them against mine. A moment in war. That's all it was.

The train back. Poplars, I guess, standing bare like a row of sentinels, a flock of birds – too far to know – passing in front of clouds lit from below and silvered underneath, a track leading to a copse and a house with a red-tiled roof, clouds – I do know those – low and high, of that world where I spend more and more of my time, shall spend all my time, maybe, and now the sun sudden from beneath the near horizon, bright but subdued at this time of year, its batteries low from its attempts to heat the fields. Water standing in furrows, lengths of wire separating larger fields, all the while the rattle rattle rattle of the carriage and the bogeys der-dum der-dumming as if they are a part of my being somehow. The seat's springs balancing me, the sun pushing the trees' shadows long, grasses at fields' edges colourless, full barns, cows moving as slowly as churches, farmhouses with their small windows, a wide river gliding between the arches of a bridge, swans like queens in barges, a station stop, porters swinging bags of mail, whistles and flags, steam passing the window, stubble, wires undulating from pole to pole as if tracing the flight of a woodpecker, another train's close bump of air, doves on a roof, lanes and lanes and lanes, a buzzard gliding high and slow.

1. Tailwheel – Locked
2. Gyro – Set
3. Generators – ON

She wouldn't let me down. 60. 70. 80. 90. 110. Pull back. Wait. Some men pray at this point. There. That realisation that I am in the air. It always makes me fill my lungs a little more. I am flying. It's that moment on Tullock's Bridge. That suspension. Climbing now. Up. And she's holding steady, the engines throbbing and zzhuzzhing, the instrument panel indicating levels and pressures as Death readies itself at heights where even the cold takes on its guise.

We emerge number one in the high squadron, coming to the surface as if from dark water, and then we see the others breaking through, their tailfins first, large dull fish suddenly plated gold by the sun. Someone says *Wow!* on the interphone, *would you look at that!* Not many people get to see such wonder. Thirty-six forts in formation moving gently in the currents.

We invariably approach the field from the south-east, and the sight of the triangle of grass and the runways which look like a giant 'A', always seem to lift the ship several feet. The standing bays look like globules of sap clinging to branches. The farms are small and the fields to the west of the tower bunch up like waves breaking into a bay. Carts and bicycles come into view between the hedgerows in the narrow lanes.

Chapter Four

George was in the yard when I pulled up. "Coffee?"

I followed him. The house was spacious Georgian grandeur. We sat at the table in the kitchen and George put a cafétière, two mugs and a jug of warm milk between us.

"So, what *does* a Head do?"

The question took me aback. I didn't know. I just did it. "Organise," I found myself saying.

"What about teaching?"

"No."

"No teaching? Well, that's a bit daft."

"I'm sorry?"

"Headteacher implies you are the head of the teachers, therefore you teach."

"It's not like that. I haven't taught for years."

"Years!"

"That's right. When you go up the ladder you leave the classroom behind."

"Doesn't make sense to me. Is that why you became a teacher, *not* to teach?"

"I became a teacher..." I stopped. "I became a teacher because..." I stopped again. "I don't know why I became a teacher."

"Oh well, nothing uncommon about that. We all end up doing things we haven't planned."

"What did you do?"

"Family business. No question of doing anything else."

"Did you want to do anything else?"

"The only thing I've ever wanted in my life was to survive the war." He held the mug in his lap and made eye contact.

"I can imagine."

There was a pause. "No you can't, actually. I don't mean to be disrespectful, but the war was an extraordinary time. If you didn't live through it, you wouldn't understand."

"Well, for me, the war meant not having a father."

"Yes yes yes, that's awful but that wasn't unique."

"It's strange though, I missed him even though I didn't know him. I still miss him. But I've always felt as if I have known *some*thing. I can't explain it."

"I *did* have a father and I never knew him!"

We laughed.

"Good coffee," I said.

"It takes no longer than instant, really, but it's so much better. How about that box? Shall we?"

I followed George across the yard and through a door into an outbuilding. There were wooden ladders, benches, trestles, an old plough, a bob-cart and various items I didn't recognise.

"Here it is. I'm surprised it's as good as it is, but this place has always been dry."

I had expected a cardboard box or perhaps a tea chest. It was neither. It was a pine blanket box similar to the one at the foot of my mother's bed. That, too, had been made by her grandfather.

"I did say you'd need the car."

"I see why. So, how long's it been here?"

"You were a baby."

"That's incredible. And how often did mum come and see it?"

"*Very* occasionally. She came here one Sunday morning and asked if I had it still, and when I said I had, she just said, 'Good'."

"Good?"

"Yes."

"So it's hardly been touched since I was a baby."

"That's right. It's locked and she didn't give me the key."

"Oh. How am I going to open it?"

George shrugged and raised his eyebrows. "Have you come across one in her belongings?"

"I haven't been in a rush to look through anything."

"I expect it'll turn up when you do."

"But she didn't even mention this box. I've no idea what's in it."

"Well, she clearly wanted it kept safe."

George and I lifted the box into the back of the car. Its presence on the back seat made me tilt the rear-view mirror to look at it as I drove home.

There has always been a difference between *my father's photograph* and *the photograph of my father*. The first meant that it was his property. The second meant that it was detached from me, something which stood on the mantelpiece and existed in its own space. *My photograph of my father* didn't get around it, either, as it was *my mother's photograph of my father*. It was hers, firstly, and he was my father almost as an aside. I went through a period of playing chess with it, placing the coffee table in the middle of the room and the photograph on a chair opposite. I looked him in the eye as he smiled over the tops of the pieces at me. *Your move.*

The photograph shows him in dress uniform, his cap raked à la Errol Flynn. It had *been* my father. It was his gravestone, too. I would run my hands over it as if I were touching his features, that definite nose and chin, lit by the sun from the west. I imagined his name capitalised along the horizontal of a cross, an aeroplane with clipped wings, longer and more capable of flight in the shadow cast in the dewed grass behind it. I would talk to him as I had talked to him so many times, as Mum had talked to him when she thought she was alone in the house.

Hi Dad, it's me. How are you? I'm fine, thank you. I've missed you. Remember the games of chess we used to play? You always won. Do you know, Dad, I used to dream that I could fly. I used to dream that I flew with you. You'd be waiting already, hanging out of the cockpit and calling me up. Come on, come on, you've got a plane to catch! *Then I'd be next to you in the co-pilot's seat and the sun would be hard in our faces, you in shades in which I could see myself smiling, no checks, just* Ready to roll? *I'd look down at your hand on the throttles and I'd put mine on top, feel its intense heat and the*

41

might of the engines through the skin. You pushed the throttles forwards and we rolled. Here we go! *We shook in our seats, the end of the runway getting closer, everything around us shuddering, the plane's blood beating faster, faster, the wings vibrating up and down, up and down, and I'd wonder what kept them on, faster, so fast that I was afraid we wouldn't make it, that we'd go straight through the fence and hedge at the end, but you pulled on the controls and there'd be a sudden magical lift, and another, and we'd clear the hedge smoothly and went up and up and up into the light getting brighter as we climbed till it was so bright I couldn't see. The dream always ended like that. I grew up wishing that you could have taught me to fly.*

I'd hug and kiss the stone and put flowers against it, and hug it again before I walked away.

I didn't know what to do with the photograph. When Mum was alive I dare not move it from where it had always been, but now, I had to remind myself, this was my house. I could do what I wanted. I could sell it.

I didn't really expect to find the key to the box, so I didn't even look for it. It was an integral lock rather than a hasp and staple with a padlock. Damaging the box was out of the question. I left it in the sitting room and used it as a coffee table. I wasn't that concerned about getting into it at first, but as it was in front of me each time I watched the news, I started to wonder how to get into it. I decided that I would go through each drawer, each shelf in Mum's room systematically.

Standing in the doorway to her room with this in mind, I realised what an odd room it was. It could have been 1943. Much of it was from that time.

My room wasn't like this as a child. Mum would decorate it. We'd strip the wallpaper together, splash the walls with warm water and score it with the corner of the scraper, then pull it off in strips. We had a competition to see who could get the longest single strip. I nearly got one from the skirting to the picture rail. I flicked a brush of water at Mum. She picked up the bucket and, apart from throwing it at me, I couldn't think what she was going to do. She did throw it! She did! Mum, that woman who was, well, Mum! Mums didn't do such things. I remember her grin. I thought when she swung it back she'd swing it forward and spin. Ha! We were both laughing, me with that she-won't-really-but-you-never-know nervousness as I backed against the wall. I felt the impact of the explosion, my hair shocked back as if I'd dived into a pool and emerged with it slick to my head. The warm water dripped from me like blood. Mum was laughing. I laughed. Then I turned and saw the wall. It was what you'd see in a cartoon, my outline on the bare dry plaster we'd stripped the day before. It was as if a particular part of me, an inner self, had been ghosted there.

"Look Mum, look!" I laughed.

Her face changed, slowly. Something hit her now, and she sat on the floor and cried.

"Mum, what's wrong? What's happened?"

Apart from the blanket box my great grandfather made, the furniture in this room is utilitarian which, to me, is representative of the war era: brown. And that's what I think of that time. I was born in a brown place in a brown time. When I watch a World War II film, even when it's in black and white, there is always a brown tint to it, as if what's on screen is suffused with weak tea.

I open the wardrobe doors and Mum's perfume clouds me. It's not unpleasant, not a smell you might associate with 'older' people. It's the smell I have always known. Feminine. I used to hide in here as a boy, behind the skirts and dresses, and the shoes arranged neatly in the bottom. My giggles would give me away. Now I part the clothes as if the key will be dangling on a ribbon. Then I take the neatly stacked clothes from the shelves and separate each garment on the bed. Nothing.

The dressing table. An embroidered piece of linen on its top, with a hair brush, hand mirror, ring tree and a studio photograph of me pulling on a sock. Two drawers. Underwear in the top, soft woollen pullovers in the bottom. I put everything on the bed. Nothing.

Bedside table. A lamp. Spectacles. The drawer, pens and bookmarks. Nothing.

The blanket box with its ribboned key. Sheets and blankets. Nothing.

Nothing.

Nothing.

I put everything back as neatly as I can.

43

The bed is sad. The only time I know two people shared it was when I had a nightmare or was ill and needed comforting. Mum would rub my legs when I had growing pains and I would eventually stop crying. Then she'd turn her back to me and I'd snuggle in. She would usually fall asleep again before me.

It's sad because she slept in the middle of this double bed. She didn't believe in quilts. It was sheets, blankets, counterpanes. *Funny things*, quilts. On the coldest winter nights she had a heavy woollen blanket on the bed, squares knitted from leftover balls. *It's like looking down on the good earth*, she said, *all these different fields*. There were acres either side of her.

Perhaps that's where the key was, buried in a field. The urge to find it waned. I had no idea what was in the box and thought it couldn't have been that important if she had removed it to another location. It might just have been in the way, and it was reasonable to lock it if it were to be kept somewhere else for a length of time. It could wait.

If Mum had known I spent time at the air base she would have skinned me. When the war ended the base reverted back to farmland. The buildings were a great place to play. We'd run down the runways with our arms outspread making aeroplane noises, dog-fighting or attacking a go-cart we'd made from which a 'crew' pointed their sticks in all directions at the single engine fighters *nee-owing* past, *doo-doo-dooshing* to replicate the sound of cannon and machine-gun fire. The Americans shot the control tower to hell when they left but from there we still managed to talk down battle-damaged bombers with three engines out, rushing out on carts to put out the fire or stretcher the injured away. We could be pilots, gunners, navigators, engineers, medics. Boys, and girls, if there were any around.

Chapter Five

14th April 1942

I am the aircraft commander but there is nothing I can do to ensure the safety of the crew. If Death wants them, Death takes them. I do my duty and am seen to be doing it, so the men at least feel as if I have their interests at heart. If my duty makes them feel secure, good, but it doesn't alter the fact that Death is beyond us, extra-ordinary. It isn't that I don't care about the men, it's that I know that my actions will not determine their fate. I have grown up with Death walking and talking and dining and diving with me. Marty had gone just like that.

What I don't understand is why, at the point at which he died, Marty woke up. He had never shown any interest in girls, not what *I* would call interest. Not the interest I had in girls. Although I was second best as far as the girls were concerned, I was happy to be. No matter. Marty was my babe magnet. I was the booby prize.

I fly in a dangerous environment; Marty was crossing the street. I dodge bogies; Marty got in the way. I am intact; Marty was broken.

There had been so many times when girls' hormones had wanted to dance with Marty's before they realised his weren't dancing. Mine were jitterbugging for them. Even for May Winke who was Marty's undoing. I thought of her as Death incarnate for a while but that was unfair. She was merely an onlooker. I have learnt that there are circumstances surrounding every death to which folks will point to explain the moment. *If only such and such didn't happen*, then he or she would be standing here now. No they wouldn't, actually there is nothing that could have been done. That *if only* was an essential component of the moment. It's a moment as complex and beautiful as the insides of a watch. There are cogs which turn, a wheel which balances. The moment is merely part of a tick-tock on the way.

It's unusually quiet on Saturday morning. You can step off the sidewalk and not have to look up and down the street before you cross. May Winke is a looker but she's never looked at me. She has just moved into the area and is sweet on Marty. She's been through me to find out about Marty just like many other girls have done: Is he going steady? Where does he hang out?

She's on errands in town this morning because I've told her that Marty and I go fishing at Tullock's Bridge Saturdays, then take our catch to Herman's for breakfast. It's become one of the things we do.

One morning we were tripping through town when Herman came out of his place and greeted us with *Boy oh boy oh boy, let's have those beauties for breakfast.* Marty held them up, still with enough sparkle from the river that they gleamed between us. It was a great breakfast. The most wonderful I've ever had, and from then on we always passed by Herman's whether we'd been lucky or not. We shared something unspoken. Later I looked upon it as our Saturday morning magic.

We had caught three that morning and it was going to be a good breakfast. One each. Herman was going to love these babies. He held up his arms like an opera singer receiving wonderful news, then put them on the slab behind the counter where he prepared them deftly with sharp knives. Herman would ask us where we caught them exactly, and how. We'd tell him the pool or the run, describe the overhanging trees under which we had to cast, the take. Each detail made the flesh sweeter and more delicate in our mouths. The taste of Tullock's Bridge. We sit a while before we take the coffee which Herman gets from somewhere secret out of town.

When we leave with rods in hand and bags slung across our shoulders, I see Marty's lace is trailing. He props his rod against a pillar and goes down on one knee to tie the lace. I see May Winke the other side of the street.

"There's May," I say.

Marty looks up and she waves to him. He smiles, stands and says, "Hey May!" stepping onto the road as one truck goes up the road and one down. The nearest clips him into the air in front of the other. It's quick and horrible. May Winke passes out.

The following Saturday I don't fish but stroll to Herman's where we sit under Marty's rod on the wall above the table. Lace, wave, truck. Such and such and such.

Since then I have seen Death deal with men more cruelly, their heads blown off, their bodies ripped apart or blown to atoms. The truck under which Marty fell crushed and mangled him. His limbs were set at odd angles. The truck drivers sat on the sidewalk, heads in hands, shaking under the coats of passers by. Marty lay crumpled in the road. I knelt beside him and knew he was already fishing a different river. *What's it like Marty? Is there a bridge?* I had known in the instant between the first truck and the second truck that he would die, because his flight was so ridiculous. *Wave Marty, wave.*

How like a doll he looked, as if tossed to the ground in careless play. I knelt next to him, then sat, pulled him onto my lap and cradled him in my arms. Hugged him and kissed him and cried. A small town Pietà.

May Winke avoided me after that so I went to her home to tell her that it wasn't her fault. It was how Death worked: she was merely a jewel in a watch movement. "You're weird," she said. So I never talked about such and such again. The men who survived when another man died found it easier to call it fate – *Que sera sera* – or marinated in copious quantities of alcohol. Herman put a photograph of Marty holding up a Beaut on the wall beneath the rod, beneath which he had written, *A good fisher.*

There is something fascinating in being attacked by enemy fighters. They are beautiful. The Me109 has a nose as sharp as a shark's snout. I record it with my memory camera, coming from a twelve o'clock position, its wings sparking cannon fire. Then it zips within feet to the next ship. I recognise the pilot as it passes under our nose. He waves, having riddled our fuselage, as if to say, *Yes, Death is up here.* Even disguised with goggles and helmet, I can see it's Marty.

If I hadn't told May Winke that Marty and I went fishing every Saturday morning. If I hadn't told her we breakfasted on our catch at Herman's. If I hadn't seen her. If I hadn't told Marty.

Not even in the National Gallery could I shake this off. If anything – *if* again – it compounded the feeling. I was no mathematician, couldn't possibly contemplate the how-many-millions-to-one-chance there was of a girl waving to a boy who bounced between two trucks which happened to pass in the road at that precise moment. Millions. In the high European air, such and such and such and such and such.

I first met him on one of my lone jaunts to look over the ship. I saw something moving against the hedge but couldn't make out what it was between the leaves and the darknesses which met and deepened there. It didn't help that he had a dog alongside, which at first suggested a several-legged creature of the night. As my eyes adjusted to these blacks and greens, I made him out, walking along the field's boundary. Although surprised to see me, he was casual in the way he touched his cap and nodded. I nodded back. In the time it took me to check over the ship he was coming back along the fence.

"You one of these fellers?" he said pointing to the ship.

"Yes."

"Bit hairy up there, I bet."

"You bet."

"Must be hard sometimes."

"You never know."

"You're right there. If it's time, it's time. Nowt you can do." He touched his cap again. "Well, pleasure talking to you." He disappeared into the darknesses at the edge of the field, then emerged from them again. "You ever seen one of these?" He opened his jacket, inside which a rabbit hung from a tab.

"Yes."

"You ever eaten one?"

"Can't say I have."

"Good eating. You come round my place and the Missus will cook it up for us."

"Why not."

"That's it. You know Four Oaks? That's our place there." Then he held out his hand: "Jason, pleased to meet you."

Chapter Six

I am facing the wrong way on the train, looking out at the half-light of dawn. The moon is full and bright, treelines rise and fall, hedges curve away like hastily drawn lines, and as the train takes a bend and straightens, the moon moves from one window to the next then back again, the glass doubling it as if one attends the other. The sky lightens and blues, the fields green and brown. The moon flashes in standing water or snags in trees. I get lost in thought and when I become aware that I have been and look out the window again, the moon has gone. Perhaps it has been flown away. Then it appears. All of this is coming over my shoulder and disappearing as soon as I recognise it, out of reach before I have a chance to consider it before something else appears.

I have the Flying Fortress in one hand and the Thunderbolt in the other. The Thunderbolt is quite insignificant, small and, being plastic, very light. Again, I don't paint the parts before assembly, so that when the colour does go on, the cockpit under the canopy remains the grey of the plastic kit. It looks bad against the rest of the model. I remind myself that I'm not a modeller. With a model in each hand I try to think of them in the same air space. It's what men of my age did when they were boys.

I catch myself in the hall mirror. I look ridiculous with a plastic kit in each hand. The Fortress hasn't even got a pilot. I have been pilotless all my life, bumbling from one safe place to another within safe distance of my mother.

When I pick up the other Flying Fortress from the model shop, I'm eager to get it home just to see its pilot. It turns out he's the same as in the Thunderbolt. I could have just bought any Airfix model of the same scale, and just popped it in the cockpit. But it wouldn't have been *the* pilot for *that* aircraft. How pathetic.

It's also pathetic that it's only now that I'm looking for my father. I did what Mum wanted. I did little to upset her, even as a teenager. I went home drunk a few times, when she'd said, "You bring trouble home and you can sort it out yourself." At fifteen I discovered that I could drink large amounts of alcohol, specifically beer. A man who could hold his beer was something. I was a natural. Not the yard-of-ale kind of drinker, more your twelve-pints-and-no-hangover drinker. I was a sound young man.

There are whole fields of frost with bare trees standing in them, low hedges like hurdles, barns pinked by the rising sun. There is magic here, beauty unexplained. There is also a moment when you realise that not-quite night conjures day. I have given myself to trying to identify that moment but it's impossible. It happens and I only know afterwards. The clouds have pink underbellies.

There is a woman in a field with a lurcher, which starts to run as the train comes along, extending its stride to full stretch, its ears back, its mouth open. Level with it, I sense its heart pumping in the deep keel of its chest and it's close enough to the fence to see its broken coat flattening against its body as it bounds. The train passes and the dog eases up, gives the train a last glance and turns back to the woman.

If I did, I can't remember the time when I resigned myself to staying with Mum. Maybe I did, maybe I didn't, an expression which in itself has an unsatisfactory hiatus in it. I am aware now of weakness in my character. I could have cut the apron strings but was happy with my situation. I have always been comfortable, never wanted for anything. Mum did her thing and I did mine. I drank in the pub, occasionally had a heavy night. No attachments.

The spirited girls with whom I'd grown up left the insularity of village life as soon as they had the chance. Mum was my geographical area, and to realise in late middle age that this was the case, that I had lived a life empty of that love which would have filled that maybe-I-did-maybe-I-didn't gap, was, well, something I couldn't express. I had accepted it all for her sake. Losing my father had impacted on me. Now I started to resent her. She should have pushed me away, encouraged me to leave. Fly the nest! She had been terrible for not doing so. Instead she had been happy to stew in her widowhood and needed my presence to stir it as well as make me feel responsible for it. The constant reminder of my father. She wouldn't let him get away again. Hers forever.

But it was easy to think all this, to blame someone else for my life. What was I doing? I was an intelligent man. I could have done whatever I wanted. I could have. I could have gone. But I didn't. I was responsible for my own way. I had the strength of character normally associated with a glove puppet.

I am the only person on the platform. It's mid evening, early winter. It's been raining and there is water standing in shallow puddles. The screen says the train's on time and I have quarter of an hour to wait. I stand with a bag on my shoulder then walk up and down the platform kicking my heels. The shelter – a glorified bus stop – speaks of drunks and urine. I think about why I didn't think 'piss'. I fear I might be that person with whom I associate such unpleasantries.

I've always had this inner sense of decorum. What would Mum say? I wanted to please everyone. What it all came down to, though, was to please me. There was no need to be coarse even if one occasionally had coarse thoughts.

The train comes in and I board and take a seat at a table. Another train pulls alongside and I look into the lit carriage at the lives entrenched in small personal spaces. There is a man with white hair, a pencil moustache, red tie, white shirt. He reminds me of someone. He smiles at me, nods. I nod back. Then my train pulls out and I'm looking at my reflection. If I cup my hands round my face I can see the track like a strip of pewter. A level crossing with flashing lights and cars waiting at the gates. Another station then, deserted. I have always liked the serrated edge of the platform roof. Industrial units, so often a feature of derelict ground near stations these days, have dull amber lights over their back doors. I feel well off, suddenly: if I were out there I'd be confronted with something that might threaten my mortality. I'm thinking motiveless murder. All from a light above a door. I used to look out of my bedroom as a child and watch the rain lashing past the amber street light. It's a similar feeling. I'm safe.

"Were you having an affair?" I hadn't planned to say it. It was a sudden possibility I verbalised, almost as a thought made audible. The reply was calm and immediate.

"I suppose some would regard it like that."

Chapman had never been to the house. Not while I was there, anyway. I regarded my mother as a virgin remade. I thought she must have had sex a handful of times with my father, then nothing since. I had no inkling that my mother had any kind of relationship other than with me.

"How long?"

"About a year after your father died."

"Bloody *hell!* So why didn't you ever get married? Why didn't you become my father?"

"Your mother never wanted it. She said she couldn't do it again. She didn't want to risk going through it again."

"Did she love you?"

"I loved her. She said she would never say that she loved me, even if she did."

"You weren't worried by that?"

"I loved her."

"So why didn't I ever know?"

"It's what she wanted. She didn't want me anywhere near you. You were your father's child."

"I don't understand. I could've had a father."

"You had a father. She said you didn't need another."

"I could've done with a father." I was listening to myself saying these things and not quite registering that I sounded like a mealy-mouthed moaner. *I could've done with a father.* What an odd thing to say. It was met with silence. "You could've helped us out."

53

"I did, all the time. Until you started work that is. Your mother wouldn't hear of it after that."

Now I was embarrassed. I had assumed Mum managed to buy me things because she was shrewd with money. Now I thought, racing bike: George Chapman; swimming lessons: George Chapman; textbooks: George Chapman.

Chapter Seven

27th April 1942

"She won't 'urt you," Jason said, as the dog nuzzled the palm of my hand. He called her away.

"It's very kind of you to invite me to dinner."

"Bit of 'ospitality. You boys are a long way from home."

We sat at a large wooden table in the kitchen. "Say, what kind of a dog is it?"

"She's a cross. Greyhound and collie."

The dog spread itself out next to the range, its ears flicking occasionally. "How much of this land's yours?"

Jason laughed. " 'ear that," he called to his wife, "feller thinks this is all ours!" He turned to me again. "None of it, it's the estate's."

"The 'estate's'? So what do you do exactly?"

"Do? Oh, this and that. Gamekeeper officially."

I must have looked blank.

"I look after the birds. Pheasants, and some partridges, too. Lovely little bird, that. Keep down the vermin. But this war's messed it up, for now anyway. So I 'elp out round and about."

"Is that what you were doing at the base?"

"Nope, just out for a stroll."

"And the rabbit?"

"Can't 'elp it if the dog runs up a rabbit." He looked at me and I could feel a smile breaking on my face as one did on his.

It's the flora of the higher atmosphere, which blossom briefly in a way one might expect in the heavens' environment, a sudden bursting bloom of crimson surrounded by grey-brown petals, its suddenness shocking the ship as if it has been taken aback by such beauty, or jostling her when several bloom in close succession, rattling us with their hot pollen. *Fliegerabwehrkanone* is an exotic German flower, 'flak' is a monosyllable of death.

"Now you sit there, you two, and I'll fill you up." She put a large plate of food in front of us both, much more than I expected.

"That looks good but it doesn't look like a rabbit," I said.

"Missus didn't want to put you off."

"I don't understand."

"Nor me, but there you are," Jason said, raising his eyebrows.

"I've seen my share of–" I hesitated because I didn't know how to say that I'd seen men made into the gravy of themselves – "unpleasant things."

"Spect you have, spect you have," she said.

"But it's kind. Thank you."

We had cleared our plates and Jason mopped up the sauce with bread, some of it catching on the point of his chin.

"You know," I said, "it's marvellous you can eat what's in the fields around you."

"And the garden," Jason said.

"Certainly stretches the rationing," she said.

"Mind if I have a look in the garden?"

"Please do, but mind the path, it's uneven."

I don't know why I asked to see the garden. I wouldn't actually know a potato from a tomato plant. I wanted to get out of the close kitchen. It felt smaller than my cockpit. I stood at the bottom of the garden and saw someone going in the back door. I didn't know one plant from another, except a few rose bushes stark against the greens. At least I could say something about them when I went back in.

"Excuse me," a voice said, "would you like to come in for pudding?"

I turned.

"Oh my God!" She put her hands to her mouth. "My God!"

"You've been a long time in the cloakroom," I said, calmly, amused to see her.

"I, I, I...didn't mean anything by it."

"Of course you didn't. Just relieve a dull Yank of his combat pay."

"No I didn't. It was Cynthia. I had to go along with it."

"You always do what Cynthia – whoever she is – says?"

"You don't know Cynthia," she said seriously.

"I don't wish to."

"Of course not. I, I...oh my God! Dad said he'd invited one of the boys over when he came back the other night. It's you!"

"Last time I looked."

"You know it's so. So strange."

"Strange."

"No, no, I mean yes, I mean of all the boys. I never thought."

"What are the chances, eh?"

"That's right, I mean."

"What's for pudding?"

"I beg your pardon?"

"You asked me would I like pudding."

"Oh. No idea. I just got home and Dad asked me to call you in."

"Let's go then."

"Don't let on, will you. Please don't."

I offered her my arm and she backed off. I smiled and nodded. Then she took it.

I can actually see the house when we pull the ship into the air, one of the thatched roofs planted in the brown earth. Its garden stretches away from the house down a gentle incline against the lane.

"I see you've met Gail," Jason said.

"Yes. You didn't say you had a daughter." I paused and she looked at me anxiously. "Such a helpful one too. You English are so polite. Feels as if you're going to steal our gums and leave our teeth behind without us noticing."

Gail turned away.

"Oh we're polite all right. Gail's a secretary so she's used to dealing with business types and the likes."

"Is that right?" I turned to her.

"Yes, at Chapman's in the village."

"Chapman's?"

"Practically own the place. All sorts of businesses. The pub, the garage – though that's a no-no at mo – the butcher. Even the bicycle shop. Churchyard's full of 'em."

"Excuse me?"

"Generations, you know, buried in the church grounds. Chapmans everywhere. Go back 'undreds of years."

We were walking along the lane from Four Oaks when an owl started up from the ground in front of us.

"It's like a floating breath," Gail said.

It had something in its talons. It looked at us from a post then flew soundless across the field. Gail turned to look at me and smiled. I didn't think about kissing her I just did. I pulled her against me.

"It's a barn owl," she said.

"I kiss you and you say it's a barn owl!"

"Yes, a barn owl." She laughed.

I hugged her and pulled her head into my chest and smelt her hair.

"I love barn owls," she said.

"It's a shame we don't fly as silently."

"Wouldn't that be good. Imagine if your wings went up and down like that!"

"Silent engines would really be something."

"I can hear your engine," she said, her head against me. "It's going like the clappers."

"I wonder why."

"Do you think about where you drop your bombs?"

"Sometimes. Usually I'm thinking about what the men in my ship are thinking."

"What *are* they thinking?"

"They're praying to whatever it is they think'll get them home. Their loved ones."

"So who thinks about you and what you're thinking?"

"No one," I said, but was thinking, perhaps Marty does.

Chapter Eight

"I brought you this." George Chapman gave me a carrier bag.

"Coffee?"

"Look in there first," he said.

I opened the bag and took out a box. It was a cafétière. "Ha! Well, thank you Mr. Chapman."

"George, please."

"That's very kind. Thank you."

"There's some coffee too," he said, handing me a packet. Then he showed me how to make it. "You found the key?"

"I've looked everywhere for it. Turned Mum's room upside down."

"She would have put it somewhere safe. It's here somewhere."

"I'm not worried. It'll turn up."

"Would've broken into it if it were mine!"

"I think my great grandfather made it. There's another just like it in Mum's room. Be an awful shame to break it. Perhaps a locksmith could get into it."

"They'll just drill straight through the lock."

"Really? At least it would only be the lock. Be a shame to damage it at all, though."

"What do you think's in it?"

"No idea. Nothing comes to mind. *You* were Mum's secret!"

"Suppose I was."

"Shame. Tell me, did Mum ask you for anything?"

"Oh no, not directly anyway. She would say something like, you could do with something and I'd offer her money and she'd say, thank you,

you're very kind. That sort of thing. I was happy to help out. Closest I ever got to family."

"Thank you. For everything. Mum must have loved you. Wish I'd known. Wish I had."

"She never said so. She said that as soon as she said it to your father, he never came back."

We sat in silence for a while, both of us with our hands around our mugs. "God, I can see how that would affect someone."

"Must have happened over and over around here," George said. "I don't think it was unusual, at all, but Gail couldn't take it."

"Do *you* think she loved you?"

"I like to think so. Just wish she'd actually said it." George looked at me.

"I'm sure she did. What I do know about Mum is that she couldn't do anything unless she felt strongly about it. I mean, true. She had conviction, if that's the right word."

"Hmm. Yes, I think you're right."

"I didn't know about you, did I, but you were together, so to speak, for years and years and years."

"She was very good at keeping things separate. Very good indeed."

"She loved you. She must have. People don't do what Mum did without love. It could hardly be regarded as merely convenient for all that time. She felt it even if she didn't say it."

George thought about it, looking into his coffee, glancing around the room.

When I hang the models from the ceiling the kits take on a presence which is significantly different from just holding them in my hands. It might be because they are becoming separate entities without relying on me for their animation. I look at them and feel excitement. I imagine them in the sky. I've tilted them so they look as if they're evading enemy fighters or changing course. I think of the men on board. A cocky fighter pilot, the little guy squashed into the ball turret under the Fortress. The moment bursts when I remember that there is no crew in the kit. Why didn't the model makers provide a crew? There should be ten little men.

It would be something, even if they were plastic.

Then I am mildly self-conscious. A man in my position shouldn't really be, one, making such things and, two, hanging them from a ceiling. I relax. No one is going to see them. My modelling skills don't look too bad now.

"I expected you to be angry when you found out about your mother and me."

"Angry? Yes, I suppose I should be."

"I would. If I'd been in your shoes."

"Yes, you're probably right. But anger is so negative. Wouldn't make anything better. Or different. And she still would've been Mum. She was always good to me."

"Aren't you...*hurt?*"

"I don't understand."

"Well, you never married. Your girlfriends haven't lasted long."

"They've tended to think that I was too close to Mum."

"What do you think now?"

"No doubt. They were right but I didn't mind."

"Really? Please, forgive me for speaking like this if I'm out of turn, but don't you *really* mind? Your mother had me all this time and you are happy to know that?"

"I didn't know so it doesn't matter."

"It does. It happened. Don't you feel cheated?"

"Not cheated."

"Not cheated? Do you *like* women?"

"What do you mean?"

"Even your mother thought you might be homosexual."

"What?"

"Because your girlfriends didn't last long."

"They didn't last long because they thought I was too close to *her*! She was why they didn't hang around! They said I was already married!"

"You're not homosexual?"

"No."

"I wondered too, I must say."

"For heaven's sake, just because a man lives with his mother doesn't mean he's gay."

"Of course not, I'm sorry."

We stopped talking. George went to the sink where he rinsed his mug and looked out of the window onto the garden. I wanted to tell him to leave that to me.

"It's not news," I said. "I know people have thought I'm gay. I don't mind, actually. It wouldn't matter if I were as far as I'm concerned, but I'm not. I felt a loyalty to Mum. That's all. Perhaps, in the light of what's turned up recently, it was misplaced. I have been made a fool of to some degree. But what the hell. No one's died. Besides, I've never actually felt that strongly about the women who came my way."

"Really? Not at all?"

I shook my head. "Not really."

"That sounds somewhat uncertain."

"No then. No."

"I'm sorry," George said. "I'm sorry for all this time. It was wrong. I should have got to know you."

"You said you couldn't."

"That's right. Gail said that there was absolutely no way that she would marry me."

"No need to apologise then."

"Still, I feel it was wrong."

"It's not a question of right or wrong. It was what you did."

"I loved her. She set the rules. But talking to you now I realise how wrong she was to have created such boundaries. We could have had time together."

"I was always envious of the boys who talked about doing things with their fathers. They sounded like the best friend you could have."

"There you go. I'm sorry."

"We can be friends now," I said.

"Yes, we can be friends now."

Chapter Nine

16th June 1942

From the lanes it must look as if the Forts are growing out of the wheat. Four engines turning over, the long grass behind like fast moving water. The trees bend.

I pull her thirty tons into the air. 10,000 feet, oxygen masks on. We climb 300 feet per minute, level out at 25,000 feet: five miles. There are ships above and below, left and right in beautiful formation. The vapour trails are like hall runners. We are one of thirty-six forts, 360 men with another delivery. I never tire of looking down on other ships which are themselves above the clouds. We are the fauna of the high air.

Enemy coast, steel helmets, tight formation. Houses, roads, fields and waterways just like England. Flowers. Sudden. Startling. A dark centre and a powdery punch of petals. There. There. Now. And now. A spray tossed in the air at a wedding. Then sound. Buffeting. The frame juddering. Lifting in my seat. It takes a long time to realise. Hundreds of brief brown clouds. Shouting over the interphone. Judder. Judder. All okay. Thighs tightening. Formation. Keep it tight. Feet on the pedals. Level. Good. Judder. Good. Flak. Flak. It's flak.

Formation. Tight legs, arms. Keep head and eyes moving. Stratoform clouds. Over to you bombardier. Autopilot. Come on come on.

Then it's like looking down on trout from above, their camouflage blending with what's beneath them, FW90s rising to meet us. To the rest of the crew they are Death incarnate. A squadron of them twirl around us, crossing currents and bursting out of eddies to take us by surprise.

2,500 rounds per minute. Gunter-gunter-gunter from all stations…gunter-gunter-gunter…gunter-gunter-gunter.

Now they're mobbing us like ravens – gunter-gunter-gunter-gunter-gunter – they can fly, I can fly – gunter-gunter-gunter-gunter-gunter – but they don't know what to make of me – gunter-gunter-gunter…gunter-gunter…gunter-gunter-gunter.

I liked the position of the church, on a rise in a clearing by the river. It could be seen from afar. You could walk down to the water where groups of people were washed of their sins periodically. That church like a stiff white cloud on a hill.

Marty and I had been scouting up the river for likely pools come spring. It was so cold our faces felt as if they'd been slapped. The water ran clear. Marty and I were excited by bare trees and water which – to those who didn't feel fish – looked like a world devoid of any form of life. They would become canopies of shade under which trout lingered in the current, rising to take whatever creatures fell from them.

We crossed the river at Tullock's Stones where Nanci Rubino and Susie Schreiner were tossing small sticks into the water. They lit up when they saw us, pushing each other and laughing.

"Hey," I said. "Never seen you here."

"I come down a while and watch my daddy fish," Nanci said.

"How about you Susie?"

"Uh uh, not me. All sorts of creepy stuff."

"You can't call Marty creepy!"

"Don't be touchy," she said. "I don't mean you."

"That's okay then," I said. Marty hadn't said a word. He was like a mute shadow.

"Say Marty, what you been up to?"

"Just looking."

"What's to look at?"

"Fish."

"Fish?"

"Yeah, fish."

"We fish all up and down this stretch, like your daddy," I said.

"Kinda strange, though, don't you think?"

"Not to us," I said.

"Well, how's about Marty telling me."

"He's right, not to us."

"It's cold, Nanci," Susie interrupted. "We should be getting back."

"Oh come on Susie, we can yak in the church out of the cold."

Perhaps it's my fault. I tease Death each time I put on my boots and jacket and helmet. Come and get me, you son of a bitch, I say, though it never sounds genuine, somehow. Death is out there, breathing the cold high air without the need for an oxygen mask. In its desperation to nail me it merely looks as if it's trying to punch holes in the sky to whatever's on the other side.

It's remarkable how warm the church is compared to the breeze that pinched us along the river. I think it's the plump cushion of darkness. I stand near the altar and watch the candles' flames register my presence. Nanci stands hard against me. "This is better, isn't it?" she says.

"I like it in here," I say. I get lost in the blue centre of the flames.

The way Nanci rubbed my trousers, unbuttoned the fly, flipped me out and took me in her hands suggested a practitioner. I had only ever kissed girls. Long kisses with tongues so that mouths had been sloppily lipsticked with saliva. In the future, would-be fighter pilots joked about joysticks and girls who could pilot them any time. Perhaps it said something about my particular tastes that I had always wanted a control column. My 'joystick' in her mouth as far as it would go, one hand in the small of my tummy and the other steadying me. I ejaculated onto the boards between the pews as the candle flame flickered on the altar and I produced a sound I had not heard before.

"Ooh, you needed that, didn't you?" Nanci said.

It was not something I ever *felt* that I needed but I have felt that I *have* needed it many times since.

Marty was at the back of the church with Susie, just kissing, he said.

"What was Nanci doing to you? You made one hell of a noise."

I didn't know, exactly, but said, "Loving me, Marty." Afterwards I felt that whatever it was, it wasn't love, but for a week or two I thought Nanci was a doll.

"Sure made a lot of noise," Marty said.

Gunter-gunter-gunter. Bombers lurch away from 109s' flaring wings and noses. Gunter-gunter-gunter. Parachutes drift like seeds in the high currents. Guts splash against the windshield. Ships are going down. Gunter-gunter. Bomb bay doors open. Gunter. Twelve 500lb fish tremble. Gunter-gunter-gunter-gunter-gunter-gunter-gunter.

Chapter Ten

Mum spent so much time here in St. Michael's. She was christened here, attended Sunday school, learned all about the feeding of the five thousand, the Battle of Jericho, the parting of the sea and the miracle of the building itself, the walls as deep as an outstretched arm, the carved font and the tightly jointed pews. If this church is a world in itself, then the roof is the sky, held aloft by hammer beams and delicate fan vaulting. I wonder if my father made such a connection, his aeroplane's back brushing up against the roof of the world.

The air in here in winter is so still one's breath creates the Holy Ghost with each exhalation. In the summer the sun's streams show your passing like a glanced fish. Mother was married here, too. My father waited for her in dress uniform and she entered on her father's arm and walked down the aisle she had walked down hundreds of times before. I wonder if she had ever imagined the day when she would do it as a bride. Of course she did. It was part of the cycle of church: christening, marriage, death. I think of *her* proud mother and father standing by the font as the priest spilled water on her brow. What would this place have been like then? Just the same. Just the same.

I come here to be close to them both and to try and understand what it was in my mother that made her separate my father and George so definitely. This is where she said, *I will*. She must have known that he might be killed, that one day he might never come back. And when he didn't, what did she do? What did it do to her? I *know* what it did. *I* am what it did.

Chapter Eleven

23rd August 1942

Five miles up is a world between worlds. This one and the next. It is the filling in the sandwich. The mid stratum. The inlay.

It *wasn't* Marty, of course. I know that. He died in the middle of the road as I hugged him. Perhaps I was seeing what I wanted to see in my first action. Head on, twelve o'clock level. Incredible closing speed, the gunners tracking the bird as it dipped beneath us. All super-sensed slow. The blue-eyed pilot's determined gaze. The rivets in the fuselage. Thinking his tail would clip us. The swastika like a crude tattoo. The smell of spent cartridges in my mask. My lungs expanding beyond the confines of their bony cage. My grip on the column tight. Then I'm flying. I know that I'm not going to be hurt. I float in the seat, then, aware of the engines' harmony and the layers of the symphony for which I'm responsible. The ship and the guns and the crew, and my body's orchestra in tune with the whole caboodle.

Autopilot enables the bombardier to sight the target and release the fish, but I never like it. For the crew it's the time when they feel most vulnerable because it means that, flying on a constant course, we are most at risk from accurate flak. The longer the bomb-run, the worse it is. It feels to me that it's not the autopilot which keeps us up, but whatever prayers and mumblings are uttered into the oxygen masks around the ship. Autopilot takes the ship out of my hands and I have to disguise the itch to control her again. She's mine. Auto points her in a straight line and the bombardier matches the reconnaissance images with the ground he sees through his bomb sight. *Bombs away!* The ship lifts as if letting go of something profound. My hands on her again. Course for home.

Home. Marty. Herman. Tullock's Bridge. That's some distance. And it isn't home. Not now. It's a cockpit five miles up and fifty below. Only crew know. Five hours vibrating back to base through who knows what yet. Goëring's Flying Circus ready to clown around us and pick us off. At least the crew can do something about the red or yellow or checker-board-nosed aircraft which close at fantastic speeds and tangents. Gunter-gunter. Their wings flare at us. Bullets can end life in an instant or perforate a line where chunks of body tear apart. Gunter. Gunter. Gunter-gunter-gunter-gunter-gunter.

The smell of sweat in my mask. My legs and back clammy. The co-pilot ducks beneath the instrument panel. Bullets rattle through the fuselage making me aware of a broken connection between my fingers and toes. The weight of the flak jacket pulls me into the seat. I am conducting the engines, airspeed, position. A ship explodes like a star. An Me109 spirals down. Ships are burning. Death come get me. Come on, your best shot. Gunter-gunter muffled by my headset. Cartridges ejected from the ball turret of a ship above us whizz by. Interphone: *All clear Captain. All in one piece back here. Let's go home. Did you see that! Holy shmoly! I sure kicked his ass. Glad my Mom ain't here.*

I love it when she first reveals her bareness. I look at her and think how lucky I am that I *know* that I'm going to touch her. It's a breath-holding state of apprehension. And she looks so wonderful, so perfect in her underwear that I sometimes wish I could penetrate her without her removing her bra and panties. The curve of her back as it sneaks under the knickers sends a shiver through me.

I sit on the edge of the bed and she comes towards me. It is she who unhooks her bra. She who slips off her panties.

"Touch me," she says quietly.

I put my hands to her breasts and run them slowly over her ribs and stomach. "I love you, Gail."

I drop through the overcast, high and fast, cream the power, lift her nose so that she looks like a horse reined in, pull her back more and, just before touch-down, squeeze all power to the engines, drop her nose and let her glide in as if I am landing a sigh. I can make her dance.

I didn't feel that I filled the uniform when I put it on. I was skinny. I think many of us were. There had been a time before I joined up when I always felt hungry but at least that was no longer the case. I loved putting on the flying gear, the sheepskin jacket and trousers. It was our armour against the cold high air. We peeled ourselves out of it when we got back as if born again each time. In effect, we were. That first time I went into combat the 109 came straight at me and under our belly, the pilot and I making eye contact, recognising something in each other. I pissed myself with relief.

It was like being in two cocoons up there: first the sheepskin, then the aircraft itself, that bucket of metal held up by God knows what. Flying school teaches you all about weather fronts and aerodynamics and thrust and cross winds, tail winds, head winds and every other wind you can possibly think of, but it doesn't tell you about the scythe which harvests within and between the clouds.

Later the ground crew will add another successful mission to the line of 'bombs' on the nose of the ship, and the Me109s' pilots will have 'victories' added to their birds. They are symbols of glory without mention of the civilians or crews killed, the destruction of districts. They are Death's shorthand on the machines of war.

Gail says nothing but lies on her belly in front of the open fire, the flames glazing her skin. She rests on her elbows and I am almost afraid to let my whole weight rest on top of her, my cock between her cheeks. Oh how I love the skin of her back against my chest.

I entered the hut just as a staff sergeant was stripping bunks and emptying lockers.

"*Maybe Baby* and *Rootin' Tootin'* didn't make it," he said.

I sat on my bunk and wrote home. The usual stuff: *weather bad but feeling swell*. There were at least twenty homes back in the US which would shortly receive a different type of letter. We regret we regret. The usual. I wondered about bullets passing through flesh, smashed faces, jumping without a parachute, the brief knowledge that this is one's time to die, that *this* is Death.

"So, Cynthia..."

"Yes, my cousin."

"Whose side?"

"Mum's. Her sister lives in London, that's why I was there. Not as scary as it used to be."

"Scary London!"

"It is for me! It's hardly the village."

"No, it's not the village. I've seen scarier, that's all."

"I know, I know. Different type of scary, I think."

"Yes, different."

"How scary *is* it, up there?"

"I think if you asked my crew they'd say pretty damn scary."

"I'm asking you."

"Yep. Scary."

"*How* scary? Tell me."

I didn't want to answer because I didn't think it was at all scary up there. Exciting. Arousing. Tingling. But definitely not scary. Some men soil themselves but every cell in my body thrills to it. All of it.

I kiss her face and pull back her hair so that I can look over her shoulder and see the weight of her breasts upon the rug. She opens her legs and I slip inside her. She stretches out her arms like wings and I take hold of each hand in mine, intertwining my fingers with hers and alternately grip and relax, grip and relax. She makes little noises and I wait and wait and wait for her to say that she loves me. I want her to say it before I come.

I am as smart as an unfolded leaf. There are wings on my uniform chromed like an angel's. The organ's music changes and Gail appears in the doorway with a faint nimbus around her head and Jason stiff in a white shirt and smiling as if he's just learned how to smile properly. I am in a church older than anything I could imagine, marrying a girl with whom I can fly. I am going to remember this.

Chapter Twelve

I'm standing in Mum's room looking at the blanket box at the foot of the bed, the key with its ribbon dangling. The key. I take it downstairs and try it in the lock of the other box. The plates inside slide and click smoothly and the key completes a turn! I sit back on my ankles. Then put my hands on the lid and lift.

The first thing is the smell, the locked years are ingrained in the wood itself. Then I take out what's inside:

- Dress uniform
- Cap
- Shoes
- Wallet
- Photograph of a young man with a rod in one hand and a fish in the other
- Photograph of my father and nine other men under the nose of a Flying Fortress
- Photograph of my father outside the church with a bicycle
- Letters
- A cigar box
- Photograph of a baby
- Fountain pen
- Grandfather's shotgun
- Leather cartridge belt
- Photograph of Mum on her wedding day
- Photograph of my father at the castle

- Copy of *Picture Post*
- Sealed envelope with my handwritten name on it
- Black and white mottled notebook

I am bigger than my father. I stand in front of the mirror in the hall in his uniform and place the cap on my head carefully. It's all too small and it doesn't make sense. He was the biggest thing in my life. It's as if the way I suppressed my need to find out about him when Mum was alive has caused the uniform to shrink. What a daft thought.

I angle the cap just like the photograph of my father. He looked like a film star, I look like one of those men who dress up in World War II uniforms at re-enactments I've always regarded with suspicion. The trousers are too short, the jacket is straining on my frame, the shoes are crippling. I wonder about the exact moment when that final cell came into being in my body for this uniform to have been a perfect fit. When I was growing up. Was I awake? Walking down a street? Writing a report? Listening in a meeting? Talking? On a train? I realise then, in this jacket, my father's arms are around me.

It was one of the runs we'd thought likely when we scouted up and down the river in the colder months. We weren't precious about who was going to fish which spot, it just seemed to happen with mutual respect for what the other saw when he looked at a stretch of water. There were places we both liked but there were also times when either of us would say – I want to try this place – and that would be it. That person could see something in the way the river and bank and trees came together: it was worth fishing. It's an experience thing. I could see my line arcing and looping like loose handwriting above the water before presenting the fly to the trout like an oh-so-tempting starter to a fancy restaurant meal. That's what Marty and I would talk about. When we weren't fishing we were talking about it.

Marty had set his heart on this spot the day before. Look at that. Just there. That's a lie for a Beaut if ever I saw one.

We could see it, keeping its position in the current, hardly moving, rising to whatever the current brought to it. He – we always called fish he – would move to the left or the right and take the bugs from the surface, then return to his groove in the water. We marvelled at his mottled back and sides blending with the stones and pebbles on the river bed.

Marty presented the fly with finesse. He cast up stream then let the fly go with the current so that the fly came down right on the nose. Up he came. Wham! What a Beaut! *Marty whooped.* What a Beaut!

He took Marty up and down the river and over to the opposite bank, tried to find a way off the hook in the weed waving like long grass in the currents, but Marty played him like an ace. He held him up and smiled a fish smile. Click. I told you, didn't I? *Click. Marty with a Beaut.*

All of these boys are going to get it on the same day at the same time at the same place. It will be catastrophic but they won't suffer. If Death can't get me then it takes what's close. I know how it works because I've seen it so many times. So I am wise to it. Marty was first.

I don't get close to the boys, maintain an air of detachment. The book says commanders must be respected by the crew but not so distant that they won't talk to you and not so friendly that they'll not respect your authority and decisions. But I'm okay with it. I have accepted their deaths already. I have seen their lockers emptied, bunks stripped and other crews rifling through their personal belongings for what's worth having: candy, packs of cards, letters, money. Their names will never be up in lights but they will be painted on a barrack wall.

We pose beneath our ship's nose art, a gal blowing out the words Gail Warning along the fuselage, NCOs *in the back, officers crouched in front. Back, left to right:*

Prentice Conti, New York, who didn't know whether London was in England or England in London before we got here;

Ralf D. Ronson, San Diego, California. Thinks a Fort is a car with wings. All he talks about is cars. Oh sure, I can fix it. It's the alternator *or some other dumb-ass thing. If he could nail a car, he would;*

Stefan B. Zimmermann, Winnebago, Illinois. Carpenter. He hasn't got his tools with him, of course, but he can whittle almost anything with his pocket knife. Carved me a fish;

Shaun F. Rumbel, Pennsylvania. His girl sent him a Dear John saying something like, I'm with your brother now, you know how it is;

Peter Dario, Hartford, Connecticut. He doesn't say much and when he does I have to concentrate to understand any of it;

Oscar Fott, Brookings, South Dakota. Two years of college. The navigator. He always says he can find the way to the nearest bar just by following his toes, whatever that means;

Front row:

Bob Sankt, Ozaukee, Wisconsin. Studying to be a veterinarian. They treat dogs better than us, he says;

Sidney C. Stone, Harrisburg, Pennsylvania. Folks are lawyers and he's heading the same way;

Franklin N. Broon, Macoupin, Illinois. My right hand man. Dependable and bright, but curled up inside himself somewhere.

Me.

All together now. Click. Gotcha.

We cycled a roundabout way to the village. Gail put bread and cheese and apples in the basket on her bicycle. "We'll stop on the way," she said.

It didn't look like much to me when we stopped at a gate. "It's just a field," I said.

She smiled. "We're going through it to that line of trees." She opened the gate and propped her bicycle against the hedge out of sight, handed me something to carry. "Come on."

We waded through the field's deep grass and Gail touched the tips with her free hand as if to stop it rising higher. Seeds clung to my trousers and embedded in the stitching in my shoes. We walked towards a line of trees, a bend in the river, where there was a beach of soft earth and the water rippling gently over stones. "Not many people come here," she said. "It's all ours."

"Nobody?"

"Dad showed me this place when I was little."

"It's pretty."

"When I'm here I could be anywhere."

"Where do you want to be?"

"Today, just here with you." She kicked off her shoes.

"Me too. But where have you been?"

"Oh, you know, exciting places. Dancing all night. Drinking champagne. That kind of thing."

"None of that compares to this. It's heaven. Look."

She looked up and down the river. "Yes, it is." She jumped to her feet. "Let's swim!"

"Swim?"

"You can fly but you can't swim?"

"I can swim but what about..." About what I didn't know.

She pulled her blouse out of her skirt and started to undress. She ran and dived into the water before I had the time to register that she was naked. "I win!" she shouted.

I stripped as quickly as wanting to keep my uniform presentable would allow and without losing composure, though my boner clearly gave away my excitement. Gail giggled and I ran into the water, my cock bouncing up against my belly.

"It's deeper out here," she said, calling from mid-stream.

I wanted to see her bareness in the full light of the afternoon sun. I swam to her and pulled her to me, my hard-on pressing into her, her breasts against my chest. She hung on to me as we kissed. Then she swam to the other bank and pulled herself out. I loved the way the water slipped away from her. She turned. Took my breath away. She dived. Then I copied her. I looked down at her and liked the way her arms and legs and body broke up as the light refracted through the water. Momentary jigsaws. I dived in and held her again.

"I love you," she said. "Don't go and get yourself killed, will you? Don't leave me like that."

"I won't get killed," I said.

"Promise me."

"I promise." She was happy with that.

"Picnic?"

She wasn't like the girls back home. There was a particular prettiness about her that I only associate with English girls. Not rose, as the English sometimes say, but certainly something which looked English to me. It was as if the seasons were in her face, energised by the cycling and the swimming, the sun high on each cheek.

"You look like summer itself," I said.

"Really?"

"You really do. Like a tree full of life. I think if I were a bird I'd want to nest in you."

She laughed. "You say some daft things." She picked up a buttercup and held it under my chin.

"Oh don't give me that nonsense."

"It's good nonsense."

"Nonsense is nonsense," I said.

She went to a tall plant with white flowers and pushed it over a little towards me. "Do you know what this is?"

"Let me guess, a...flower?"

"It's meadowsweet, which is good for fevers and diarrhoea. And this," she said, ranging more widely, "is..."

"Another buttercup," I interrupted.

"Look, you, I know what it is!" She touched its yellow flowers. "It's tormentil, no end of good for a sore throat." She spotted something at the water's edge. "Knitbone is good if I break your neck," she laughed, wagging its purplish flowers at me. "And water mint—" she crushed a leaf and offered her open hand to my nose – "is good for colds and indigestion."

"So what's this?" I said, taking a large spear of purple flowers from a plant.

"Purple loosestrife. It's for daft American pilots to find out, that's what it is."

"You're just making up these names."

"You'll have to take my word for it."

"Can't trust the word of a pickpocket."

"Ouch!" She was embarrassed.

"I'm sorry, that was unfair." I was embarrassed now. "How do you know all this?"

"It's what you know if you're brought up here and your father's a gamekeeper. Dad always says everything you need is around you, if you can be bothered to look."

We dried in the sun and ate the picnic under the trees before cycling on to the village. Gail put her bike against the boundary wall of the church. "Stand here," she said, pointing to a place next to the gate.

I leant against the bicycle saddle, placed my hands on the handlebars, put my weight on my left foot, crossed my right in front of it, and smiled. Click.

She took my hand then. "This is where I was christened. This is where everyone is christened. And buried."

Abutting the path were old graves. I stopped to look at their names and dates. There was a row of stones with the name Chapman going back to the seventeen hundreds, the names of sons and daughters chiselled on stones on either side.

"Come on," she said, pulling me towards the door.

"You left out something just now."

"Left out?"

"You said everyone is christened and buried here."

"Everyone."

"What about married?"

"Yes, that too."

"Will you be married here?"

"One day."

"Will it be me?"

"Is that a proposal?"

"Yes, it's a proposal."

Dearest Gail,

You will be reading this if I don't come back. First, I apologise for breaking the promise I made to you when your whole being expressed itself in a look of piercing singularity that I should always return. To imagine the look on your face as you read this now fills me with a grief as great as any I have felt.

Second, I am not dead. I am the river coursing through you, full of life that exists within and alongside it. Its source is a mountain, its solace is the sea.

What I remember now are all those times when to look at you – just look – made something within me relax and spread: when *you came to find me in the garden, when you sat by the river and breadcrumbs fell onto your breasts like flakes of snow, when you put a baby in my arms and said, Look what we have.*

Grief is for the dead only. Our child is life. Our life. Half me, half you. I love you Gail. I always shall. You were a gift to me. A full river in a full summer.

Thank you for everything.

All my love.

Gray xxx

The cigar box rattles. Inside there are two medals, one like a cameo portrait in purple and gold, the other a propeller in relief upon a cross. I take the former to be George Washington in profile like one of those Georgian silhouettes in a frame, with his hair plaited down his back, a high collar to the jaw line, coat lapel across his chest and epaulette capping the shoulder. The other medal is a Maltese cross between whose arms there is a sunburst. The ribbon is particularly striking, its blue and red and white reminding me of the French flag rather than the U.S. A flying cross. In my hand each medal is a significant weight, each a symbol of just one event in my father's life.

What does a bomber pilot *do* to get a medal? All they had to do was fly. It was the rest of the crew who did the fighting, the ones who fired guns in anger and dropped the bombs. The pilot just flew. There must have been more to it than that. Without the pilot there was no way of taking the fight to Hitler. Dad was trying to win the war and Goëring's Luftwaffe was trying to knock him down. He focused on delivering the bombs to a specific place while aeroplanes and anti-aircraft batteries tried to knock him out of the sky. Medals recognised contribution. The black and white man on the mantelpiece is suddenly heroic.

I hold him as carefully as a ticking bomb. 9½ lbs of sleep, a little whirr in his nose as he exhales, his lips moving as if he's having a small conversation in the depth of whichever heaven he is in. It would be dandy to take such peace and warmth up to 25,000 feet to foil Death's attempts to knock me down. There is something frightening in this piece of me. Death wouldn't dare.

Gail and I started from our own end of the bridge and met in the middle and made him. He swings way above the river. It's how we all start. One day, perhaps, he will stretch out his arms to either side and take hold of whatever is offered. Maybe he will go both ways.

"Will you stop kissing him and look this way!"

I look up and squint into the sun. Click.

Gail is standing in the garden and I'm on the threshold of the back door in my shirt sleeves. Click.

"One more," she says.

"I can't even see you," I say.

"As long as I can see you it's okay."

"My eyes'll be closed."

The sun splashes onto his face as I turn towards the camera. Click. Then he goes off.

The fountain pen is marbled orange-black with gold-coloured fittings, a band around the top of the cap and two others on the barrel of the pen itself. There is a white swan engraved in the top of the cap, and the clip reads PATENT JAN 19 1915. The nib says SWAN 2 14CT MABIE TODD & CO LTD MADE IN ENGLAND. There is a heart punched in the middle which feeds to each pad of the nib's blade. On the barrel it says SWAN SELF FILLER. I open the bottle of ink and dip the pen, then write my father's name with the flexible nib in blue-black ink. Each letter reveals something of his character.

Granddad's gun has been broken into its parts. I press the button on the fore-end and slip off the hand-grip, slot the barrels and boxlock together, close the breech and slap on the fore-end. I open it, point the barrels towards the window and sight through. I remember Granddad doing this. I can see the world, too, at the end of a barrel, a small circle of light.

I sling the cartridge belt low on my waist like a cowboy and pretend to draw like a gunslinger. I did this as a boy. "You daft bugger!" Granddad said, cuffing me.

I weigh the battered mottled black and white notebook in my hands before I open it to the first page. My father's handwriting:

18th January 1942
Death is afraid of me.
  I have known this since my first flight. I had watched a pair of flyers at Bower's Field and it looked easy. The pilots waved and smiled and whooped and skirled around the sky. I could do that without an aeroplane, all on my lonesome.
  I was swimming at Tullock's Steps with Marty Greenberg when I looked up at the bridge and said I could fly.

Then I flick to the last entry:

16th September 1943
One day I jumped off a bridge. One day Marty crossed a bridge. Every day I am aware of it. There must be a way of getting from here to there and when I think about it I wonder about its construction.
  Someone had a vision of it connecting the two sides, described its presence with fine pens on a huge sheet on an expansive board. I can see the ink in the paper fibres like moss in stone, cross sections of the pillars which have to be sunk deep into bedrock. Stone pillars growing stone by stone behind a skeleton of scaffolding. Then I see the pillar revealed as the scaffolding comes down. From each pillar chains suspend the bridge itself, stilling it in mid-air, anchored in what's either side. The chains are joined like the links of a bicycle, one link bolted to the other and nuts tightened by a spanner as big as a leg. There were men whose love of being on a rope swing as boys now swung in arcs and space they once dreamed of, when a fall would merely have been a dunk in the river. A fall now would be forever.
  Wherever that bridge is, I am not going to cross it. Death can throw whatever it wants at me: Me109 pilots who can hit an apple from a man's head at a

thousand yards, flak, cold. Whatever. I am going to teach Death a lesson.

I've been side-stepping Death all this time and now I know what I must do. I should have known a long time ago but I just didn't get it. Marty was the first. In trying to get to me, Death has taken whatever it can get. If it takes these crews, if it takes _my_ crew, then it will take whatever is closest to me. It will take Gail. And it will take my little bomb. I couldn't live without them so this decision isn't difficult: I must take Death away from them.

Breconshire Constabulary

Sir,

I attended a suspected burglary at Nant Farm on the morning of 16th September 1953.

Glyn Williams showed me where the dwelling had been broken into. The sash stay to the parlour window had been forced and left open. Mr. Williams believed that whoever accessed the property had entered several rooms but taken nothing.

I took a statement.

I was called again to Nant Farm on the 21st September. Mr. Williams took me to a barn on his property known as Ysgubor Gigfran. Inside there were indications that a person unknown had been living there. A bed had been made out of hay and blankets. Mr. Williams identified the blankets as belonging to him.

There was evidence that a fire had been made. There were the remains of rabbits and one hanging.

I asked Mr. Williams if he had seen anything to cause him to be suspicious. He said that the previous day he had seen a man walking on his land who was not dressed for walking. He described him as tall and wearing a jacket and tie. The man was too far away to talk.

I visited the neighbouring farms and requested they be vigilant.

I informed the Parish Council and the Breconshire Farmers and the Common Land Pasture Association.

Your Servant,
Arthur John
P.C. 282

<u>Breconshire Constabulary</u>   <u>"C" Division</u>
                                                        Police Station,
                                                        CRICKHOWELL.
                                                        27th September 1963.

Sir,

Further to reports of thefts from rural properties and
sightings of an unknown person, I patrolled the area by car on the
16th September.

I was on Lon Gigfran when a man I did not know crossed
approximately one hundred yards in front of me. He was carrying
a shotgun and moving quickly. I stopped and called to him but he
was well down the field and did not respond. I saw him enter Coed
Morgan.

He was going in the direction of Nant Farm so I drove there.
When I arrived Mr. Glyn Williams was in the yard. I told him there
had been thefts from rural properties as well as sightings of
an unknown person. Mr. Williams said that he was aware of such
facts. I told him about the person I had just seen heading in the
direction of the farm. Then we heard two gunshots which came from
Coed Morgan.

Sometime later the person I had seen emerged from the wood
carrying a fox. I indicated to the man in the field and asked Mr.
Williams if he was known to him. Mr. Williams looked surprised
when he saw this person but said, "He is my nephew."

The man walked to us and showed the fox to Mr. Williams.
Mr. Williams said that they had been troubled by foxes recently.
I asked the nephew his name. He did not speak. Mr. Williams
responded that his nephew was dumb.

No more thefts have been reported.

I informed the Parish Council and the Breconshire Farmers and
the Common Land Pasture Association.

                                            Your Servant,
                                            Arthur John
                                            Sergeant

Chapter Thirteen

Her first words – "You're a bit old for playing with that, aren't you?" – unsettled me. My response was merely to look at her perplexed. "That little man," she said, pointing to the small Airfix pilot on the table in front of me.

"It's my father," I said.

"Oh."

That was it. She took away my plate. I couldn't congratulate myself on having impressed her on that occasion and thinking about it now it's quite miraculous that she spoke to me again. I had just eaten a lamb shank dinner at the table next to the fire taking the chill off the room. I had a pint of beer and was reading a local guide book.

"You on holiday?" she said, clearing the next table.

"It wasn't the original intention, but you could call it that."

"What is it, if it's not a holiday?"

"It's a bit of a story."

"Sad or happy?"

"Both," I said.

"Somewhere in the middle then?"

"Yes." I found myself smiling.

She smiled back. "Have you come far?"

"Suffolk."

"Never been there," she said, "what's it like?"

"Like?"

"You know, *like*. Compared to here."

"I don't know, I've only just got here. It's flat, Suffolk's flat."

"Ah," she said, as if that's what she needed to know. "You been here before?"

"First time. First time in Wales, period."

"Your father?"

"He died here."

"I see, that's why it's happy-sad." She smiled understanding. "It'll be good for you to look around."

The apron she wore accentuated her waist and the turn of her ankles sparked something in me as she walked away. I wished I hadn't said *period*. An expression I didn't recall ever saying before. American.

I didn't know what I would say to the doctor. I couldn't say, *I think I need some time off to look for my father.*

"I can't sleep, I'm exhausted, I can't concentrate, it's affecting my decisions."

"Anything happen to you recently, anything to upset your equilibrium?"

"My mother died," I said.

His exhalation and bringing together of hands was the diagnosis and treatment in one. "People deal with the death of a parent in different ways. Your symptoms are not unusual. Let's not try drug therapy at this stage. See how it goes. Go away for a few days. Do you good."

So that's how I found myself in this hotel in Wales, an envelope addressed to me in my father's hand unopened in my bag.

My father crashed in Wales. Talk about lost! *I* hadn't even been there. I suddenly felt that at the age of fifty I had something to answer for. The only time I had considered Wales was when the rugby was on. In my capacity as a history teacher I had enjoyed – as historians enjoy such things – the exploits of Lloyd George, the General Strike of 1926, and the contribution of the mines to the Great War. But I'd never been there. Not that it would have made any difference to my father. It's not as if he was there to see the castles. Yet I had the opportunity to see where he died. I could find where he crossed over.

With Radio Four and the heating on, it felt quite good. I was cruising at sixty – no rush – and the way ahead was clear. Near Bristol the landscape changed, and coming over the top of a hill from the interchange with the M5, a new world opened out before me. There was a bridge stepping over the wide River Severn, hills building on the horizon in such a way that I wasn't sure at first whether they were hills or clouds. It was magical. I felt a lift. That's where my father was. Crossing the bridge I saw another being constructed further down river, a line of pillars jutting out of the water like the vertebra of an exposed creature.

Near Abergavenny I crested a hill and expected the sky to meet the earth way ahead, but it didn't, held up by peaks which prevented it from crushing the fields between them. The panorama was more than I'd ever seen and I realised how small my life had been. I was here to find my father whose life packed in more than mine even though I was more than double his age when he died. I had had everything and nothing, and apart from a school trip to Ostende when I was ten years old, I'd been nowhere. Holidays with Mum were to London to see cousin Cynthia. It all mattered now.

The Bear Hotel was on a bend looking down the High Street, though High Street was far too grand if this was the extent of the place. I drove through the archway into the hotel's courtyard.

On a wall in the bar was a photograph of a bear dancing outside the hotel at the turn of the century. In another, there was a large puddle outside the entrance into which a boy dangled a fishing line. I liked the humour. It could have been me fishing for my father. The puddle was the strange place my father inhabited within me. A dark pool. A man looked on as the boy waited patiently.

Looking back at the hotel from the High Street, the hills rose behind it. One looked like a table and was called locally, Table Mountain. The Ordnance Survey Map I bought told me it was actually called Crug Hywel. Somewhere near there my father died, and although I knew he was American, I felt that he was from *this* place. He was there. The hills challenged me to go to him.

I was used to country roads but here they went up and down steeply. The contour lines on the map were so close together that I thought there should be steps. My lack of fitness made me feel inadequate.

The tourist information office catered for walkers. There were walks of varying difficulty and length, canal cruise companies, nature guides, programmes for local theatres and leaflets for castles and museums. There was no *Where to find your father* on the racks, no walks to him, no post-card. You could buy a fluffy Welsh dragon, a miner made of coal, even a miner's lamp. There was an advertisement for guided fishing on the Usk, the Brecon Beacons Visitor Centre leaflet used a photograph of a couple standing on a rock looking out over a valley. A family at the counter was getting advice about where to go and what to do. I waited.

When it was my turn I wanted to say, *Can you tell me where I can find my father?* But it came out differently: "I know this might be an odd request, but an aeroplane crashed near here in the war and I was wondering whether you knew anything about it?"

I was woken by the sound of birds. Robin, blackbird, starling and, at a little distance, wren. I looked to the window, the curtains apart slightly, the top light open. I found these sounds familiar, especially the wren whose music was so pretty and loud for such a small creature. It must have been made by a watch maker.

The room was comfortable. I had nothing else. The roads had brought me to a different place, the ground higher, the views grander, the world larger than I had known.

The interior was what one expected to see in a BBC production of Ye Olde Inn. Brass horns, a bugle, a huge open dresser with chargers and pewter tankards, a Viennese regulator, a longcase clock, panelling, settles, window seats with cushions, a black and cream colour scheme, beams in which there were mortises to indicate old stud walls. The lighting could be described as dim. The men serving at the bar were in shirts and ties and the women all in black. The service was efficient and graceful. There were daffodils in small white bud vases and old dogs under tables.

I sat on a settle at a table to the right of the fire. I tried to understand what I was feeling. At home, oddly. There was something in my psyche playing tricks on me, something saying, *This is where you belong; this is where your father is.*

SO243253. I traced the way back from the close contour lines of the grid reference to the nearest pub and church and telephone at Llanbedr, down a steep narrow slope, a dotted track through green fir woods, yellow lanes from which white ribbony lanes led to farms outlined in simple blocks. With the map unfolded on the hotel floor, the hills looked like stepping stones to the other side of the room.

The spur to the right of the reference was Pen Gwyllt Meirch, the left Pen Garreg. The nearest high point was Pen Twyn Mawr at 658 metres. The names were nothing to me but I thought I should know what they meant. There was no great mystery, probably, most of them describing the specific geographical feature, as Four Oaks described just that back home. I guessed at meanings before I'd seen the places – Pentwyn, Ty Mawr – but guessing wasn't good enough. Everything here was important. Everything was my father in some way. It was irrational. I wasn't sifting through evidence but responding to what was around me emotionally, on a level with which I was uncomfortable. It wasn't that I believed I shouldn't respond to things emotionally, rather in that state of mind – finding my father state – I was vulnerable. I had blocked out the need for him all my life. Now that I was free to do as I wished, my stamina was questionable. I was disappointed with myself and I needed to consolidate whatever strength I did have.

The drunk man in a suit was friendly. He stood at the bar and spoke to anyone who came to order their food and drinks. When I realised he was about my age I became more interested. I couldn't remember the last time I had had so much to drink, when people might have looked at me and considered my drunkenness.

"Join me?" he asked.

"That's kind," I said, "but I've got it covered."

"Go on, it's my birthday. Let me get this one."

91

"Better still," I said, "let me get yours." He rocked back and smiled, raised his eyebrows and tumbler, nodded. The barman put another whiskey in front of him without having to be asked.

From my table I watched him. His birthday. Fifty or thereabouts, and alone, trying to make friends, something I never felt I needed to do and about which I became conscious now. I had no friends. I had colleagues but there was no one I relied on. George came to mind: was he a friend now? He was something. He was a link to my mother and a link to my father. In the hills nearby. At the end of a lane at the end of a valley. Here I go again, thinking all this in a kind of film-trailer voice echoing in my head.

"I was wondering if you'd be eating tonight," she said.

"Not tonight. I wanted to see a little more of the place, so I had a stroll and a bag of chips."

"Sounds like a good evening."

"Yes, it was."

"Good."

"You could tempt me with a coffee, though."

"I'll bring it over," she said.

I sat where I had dined the previous evening and she brought the coffee on a tray with two chocolates on a small white plate. "I only wanted coffee," I said.

"A little treat," she said, smiling. "One each. I'm on my break. That okay with you?" she said, before sitting.

"Please," I said, catching sight of her breasts as she pulled up her chair. She was wearing a V-neck, her skin like alabaster. Alabaster? Where did that come from? I didn't know, but I did know that I had an urge to kiss it. She leant on the table and her breasts pushed together, the cleavage presenting itself for my kisses. I wished.

"You going to have one? They're very good."

"I don't really eat chocolates," I said. She took one from the plate and offered it to me. "'Really eat'…? How do you eat them?"

"I mean…"

"I know what you mean, just teasing. You're probably used to high street rubbish. These are the business."

The chocolate was intense and concentrated and kept asserting itself in my mouth.

"Told you," she said.

"I see what you mean."

"Good. Now, tell me about your father."

"Your break's not long enough."

"Start now, finish later."

I took 'later' to mean that she would come back to my room when she finished work. "What do you mean 'later'?"

She looked at me. "Another time, you know. Again."

"Oh right."

The penny dropped with her. "Like back in your room, or something?"

"Yes, something like that."

"Steady on," she laughed.

I was embarrassed now. "Sorry, I didn't mean anything by it."

"It's not a problem."

"What time *do* you finish?"

"When everything's done."

"What do you do during the day?"

"Do? I work."

"Where?"

"Where do you think?"

"No idea."

"Here!"

I was embarrassed again. "I'm sorry. I just thought you worked here in the evenings."

"No I work here whenever, days and evenings. What did you think I did during the day?"

"I don't know. Something else."

"It varies. They call on me at all times."

On the back of the Ordnance Survey map is a diagram of Wales with a tessellation of numbered maps covering small areas, and the place where my father crashed is a pin-point on this sheet. A large pink section of another diagram illustrates the extent of the Black Mountains under the care of the Brecon Beacons National Park. There is also a list of what's covered by this map: Beacons Way; Ebbw Vale Walk; Herefordshire Trail; Offa's Dyke Path; Rhymney Valley Walk; Taff Trail; Three Castles Walk; Three Rivers Ride; Usk Valley Walk; Wye Valley Walk. Worlds within worlds within worlds. I feel that I need a philosopher to explain something to me but I don't know what. I need reassurance of some kind.

I had been reading in bed for about twenty minutes when I heard a knock on the door. A little louder. She did want to take the coffee further! Louder. Her waist. I got out of bed and put on my dressing gown. Ankles. Before I could get to the door she knocked again and in that instant I became aware of my body: I was shaking. Alabaster. I opened the door.

"Shorry, wrong room," the drunk birthday man said. He fell to the floor. I helped him back to his feet and he pushed me away, mumbling.

It's too much for me. My father died here and I'm going to meet him. *Hi Dad. I've missed you.* I am sitting on the bed in my hotel room and tears are running down my face. I don't understand why that sudden glimpse of her alabaster breasts comes to me then. I pack my bag and leave.

I was fifteen miles from home and the way ahead was clear. I didn't take my eye off the road. I was looking ahead but I wasn't *seeing*. I realised there was a bend and I was going too fast to negotiate it. I went somewhere. I braked and the car skidded, the weight of the vehicle piled onto the front wheels as if it was about to stand on end. I could see the hedge getting closer and the trunk of an oak getting bigger in the windscreen space. I braced. The car hit the tree, went up in the air and came to a rest slewed across the road. I sat for a moment as I realised what had happened. I was okay. I got out. I was okay. The front of the car had concertinaed. A write-off. I had gone somewhere and crashed my car into a tree. I don't know where I went. I have no idea where.

Chapter Fourteen

When I unfold the OS map for Woodbridge & Saxmundham, the airfield takes some finding. It's hard to believe that between these small fine lines – a millimetre apart – such huge machines rattled to a speed necessary for take-off. Hundreds of men on their way to uncertainty, dots moving across this page and onto another, perhaps to the page which isn't published in any format. What form would *that* take?

Compared to the crash-site map, it is largely white and contour-less, with two large green jigsaw shapes to the south – Tunstall and Rendlesham forests. The map's greatest forest is the blue of Aldeburgh Bay and the North Sea to the east. I open out each OS map – crash site and Woodbridge – and put them on the floor side by side. It is my father's crash site to which I am drawn.

This is where I played as a boy. The huts are still here but the plough goes right up to them now. Corrugated half cylinders where my father bunked down and wrote his letters and thought about Mum and flying and home. And me, maybe. Today the sky is as huge as I've ever seen it. It's clear apart from a wisp of cloud here and there. I'm conscious that 'wisp' is not a meteorological term and expect there's a technical description for it. I try to remember words for clouds. Cumulo-something. My father would have known. I wonder what else he knew.

I've never needed a map before but I need one now. It might be the way to my father or perhaps it will take me part of the way. What did my father's navigator use? Are there roads in the air? Are there road signs? What about the highway code?

When I was growing up – the first time – I learned where things were by association: a hedge, a gate, a house. I found my way around until I could get home from miles away, across fields and rivers and lanes. As the crow flies and otherwise. But what about my father's compass? Was it like a ship's, a large semi-sphere in which the compass rolled or swung around on a gimble as the ship crashed into waves and fell into troughs? I suppose the navigator plotted the course and father just steered.

The compass needle always points north. Something moves in me, floats, trembles and points to my father, but there's no chart on which to plot a route to him.

When I was about eleven years old the Geography teacher took the class out of school to make a map of the village. Back in the classroom he put the skeleton of the place on the blackboard for us to copy. The first thing each person had to do was plot their own home, then the village's vital organs: the church, pubs, post office, bank. The teacher said my map was extraordinary for its accuracy but added, "Spruce it up, lad." That was the first time I'd heard the word 'spruce'.

It was then I realised we spin in the same world. Some of the other children found it difficult to picture the village from above but I loved it. Since I dreamed about flying so often, I had seen my world from above so many times. I could delineate the outside lavatories at the bottoms of gardens as well as farm outbuildings and the precise shapes and current status of fields. I pointed out to the teacher that he had made an error on his version on the board. It annoyed him.

"What do you mean, Sir?"

"Spruce lad. Put some colour in it." He took the coloured pencils from my pencil case. "Here. The world's not black and white."

So I coloured in the world. It came back to me as I looked down on Four Oaks on the Ordnance Survey map. I wondered what came of that map I drew. I even included my grandfather's vegetable patch, telling the teacher what was what.

I look at maps now and wonder about all the times I might have used them. I've never really needed them, relying on the connections set down in memory. The way all the places I was interested in as a boy were instantly recalled. My grandfather taught me short-cuts across the land, through woods, across lanes and along rivers. There were even stepping stones. Perhaps my father is with Granddad, being taught the difference between roach and rudd or chub and trout as they shoal in the overhang of a willow.

My father turns to me: *The intercom's gone. Get back there and see what's going on.*

I leave the co-pilot's seat and go back into the aeroplane. The wind blasts through the windows where the waist guns swing, my hair flaps around my face. I'm in flying gear so heavy it feels like carrying a sheep. There are bullet holes dotting the fuselage and when I look out the window I see large holes in the starboard wing. Then I am stopped in a moment, unable to move, yet aware of all that is happening around me. The navigator is stilled, holding a pencil against a straight edge which begins at a photograph of my father and ends with a photograph of me as a baby.

The radio operator listens intently. He has one hand on the dial and writes with the other:

Go.. to.. the.. back.. of.. the.. ship.

The waist guns thump and rattle on their mounts, swinging fast up and down, left and right. Then the men appear, wholly fixed on what they can see along the barrel. *Come get some, fuckers!* The aeroplane shakes and jumps and the two gunners struggle to keep their feet on the cartridges that litter the floor. Fighters that look like distant specks buzz above or below a second later with wings flaring and their bullets schnapping through the skin of the plane.

The ball turret's whirring reverberates in my skeleton.

The tail gun points out of the back of the plane like a sting. The gunner turns to me. It's Granddad! *They're a bugger to hit*, he says. *You try.* We struggle in the small space to exchange places. I can't see anything but open sky, then something roars past before I can even register what it is.

There's one of them Messerschmitt things! Granddad shouts, and I see a speck coming straight at us bigger and bigger and bigger. *Now!* Granddad shouts. I pull the trigger and the gun feels like something wild trying to get out of my grip, bullets go all over the sky. *Let me*, Granddad says, moving back into position.

I am making my way down the plane when I'm punched in the gut and a huge red rose blooms in my jacket, then in the chest where a lily happens, and five daffodils trumpet in succession down my left arm. Granddad taps me on the shoulder. He smiles just as the aeroplane shudders and whatever comes through the fuselage takes off his head which is replaced instantly by a sunflower. He continues to stand for a moment before he sinks gently to the floor and the petals begin to peel off in the rattling wind. I struggle to the cockpit.

"Dad, it's hell back there."

"It's okay son. Just take a seat. I'll get us home."

"Where is home?"

"Where your mother is."

"She's dead, Dad."

"She was fine when I left her last night."

Through the cockpit we see a fighter coming at us level – badder, badder-badder, badder-badder-badder-badder-badder-BADDER…

Flat white. It takes a while to register that it's the ceiling. I'm wet. I get out of bed and put on the light. I pull back the quilt to reveal my body-shaped patch of sweat.

Chapter Fifteen

Railways made Britain great.

I want to board a train at my front door and be taken to the hill where my father's aeroplane lost its way and he crossed the bridge. But it isn't that easy. It's meant to be five and a half hours but I can't do that last twenty-odd minutes. An hour and thirty-eight to Liverpool Street, then the Circle Line to Paddington. An hour and forty-six to Newport, which is where I run out of steam...

I alight on platform two and cross the station to platform three to wait for the Abergavenny train. I'll get a taxi from there the half-dozen miles to Crickhowell.

The train comes in but I don't get on. There is something stopping me: the image of the hills like a wall as I emerge from the Severn Tunnel has lodged in my memory like a splinter. I can see it but I can't get it out. I try and try to get it out of there. I keep trying.

Sometimes it's consecutive days. I get to know the faces on the route, the staff. It's one of those mornings balancing seasons, when the sun appears a little earlier as if it's pushing against the dark night. The train comes to a stop on the line somewhere between two stations, a large pond on the left and open country to the right. It's possible to the see the individual stones between the sleepers bedding the way forward. The sun strikes the fence posts. It's a bucolic Victorian painting. Trees lean long across the fields, tumps and tufts fixed like waves in various states, building and breaking. The track curves behind a small hill in shade then emerges into a slash of light.

The feeling of being hemmed in continues for some time before the banks roll back to open fields when I emerge from the tunnel. Late afternoon, late April, the sun warms the glass, cows – their flanks heavy with mud – rub against fallen trees. I know when the next tunnel is coming: the light dims and the banks rise above the height of the carriage windows until it's swallowed suddenly. Then I'm trapped in the strange world between the panes of glass, a ghost in the machine. Is it my father? He's trying to contact me in the only way he knows, showing me that he's there. *Hi Dad, how are you? Can you get me out of here? Can you meet me?* He imitates my small movements. Just as I get used to my other self, it disappears in that flash of sun as the tunnel spits us out.

Gardens which a couple of weeks ago looked derelict are now something for a magazine. Borders are clear, lawns mown and lush. Rivers look as if you could drop a line in them and pull out something good to eat. Tractors turn a large field's red breadth. There are so many white lambs thickening.

A scrapyard I've seen before, cars piled up on each other, their journeys ready to be crushed, tells me I'm coming into a station. People wait to begin journeys or to meet others from theirs. A housing estate then, with plastic conservatories tacked on the backs of lives. Hell, now I'm conscious of how I'm processing all this. I am a fifty year old mummy's boy. Christ – something I could never have said in front of mother – what a catch! At fifty, though, it's more like whatever's been left on the shelf after everyone's taken what they wanted, and the key to the room has been lost.

May. The fields are green. They've been green before but now they are the green-green of summer. The hedges along the track are flush with it. The trees in the fields – if they are not full like expanded lungs already – are leafing as I imagine bronchi must. But what makes this journey full of wonder is the yellow rape, a yellow so strong it dents the eye. There is a stretch of track either side of which the yellow laps up to the train as if it's on a causeway. Then I think of the yellow as a thick layer of paint into which tractors have sgraffitoed their wheels to reveal the green under-paint. There is nothing without this green. Green is everything. A farm on a mound bobs like an ark above the fields. A river runs clear beneath a bridge. A station where gulls glide around the chimneys. The stations are stepping stones across the yellow sea.

Mid June. Heat. I have to take off my jacket. A variety of greens with sprinklers, parallel lines in the tall corn, fields of hay baled in round balls, trackside vegetation dense and encroaching. Landmarks that were distinct and sharp a week or two ago are softened by trees and bushes. A car is parked in a gateway, its occupant sipping from a cup. I'll never find my father in all this. Even the trees look as if they're out of their depths.

Swans upend in ponds and look like marker buoys. Cows sway in fields like large women stepping out, graceful and easy.

Stopping at points, my reflection in an open-necked white shirt causes me to look inward again. My head is lost in the leaves of an ash tree nearby. I'm in there somewhere and it makes me think that my father is also. Perhaps he's in the junction box. Change the points, man, change the points. There is litter on the tracks. So many journeys' litter.

Woodbridge
　..Westerfield
　　..Ipswich
　　　..Colchester
　　　　..Witham
　　　　　..Chelmsford
　　　　　　..Shenfield

I can go back to the doctor but I don't think it will achieve anything. Explaining to him that there's something stopping me from going to my father's crash site seems ridiculous to me. He might say, "And what do you want me to do about it?" I wouldn't blame him. Or he might suggest counselling and I don't want to talk about what I already know. It's just something I have to get through. Sometimes I think it's a kind of winter, a sustained period of darkness. Other times I think it's because I need my mother's permission. "All that matters is what I've told you," she said. It isn't. There's my father's journal. All those years when I hadn't wanted to upset her, I had been playing dead.

21st June. High sun. Clouds I don't know how to describe are thin and ethereal. Hay cut and filed, drying in the heat. Meadows of buttercups. Woodpigeons. I taste childhood meals with my grandfather. Buzzards on thermals. The rape's gone over. Deep green corn. The simplicity of corrugated buildings, their green and rust. A still pond with a still swan. Rooks worrying around livestock feeders. The sun silver-gilting slate roofs. A large field of potatoes. *Pommes de terre!* Local produce. Small rich-brown bullocks. Under and over stone bridges. That's it, maybe I go over and he's beneath me, or vice versa. Dad. Dad!

I've just realised that I always sit on the right side of the train, only look at that half of the world. Whatever's on the left is rarely considered, though it's always that side for the platform, watching a hundred journeys stop or break or end. Scrapyard. Windscreens and chrome bouncing the sun between them. I'm going to get off, too. What does the end of the track look like? Where does it go? Is there a bridge? Is *that* where Dad is? I'm afraid to go all the way in case I miss him somewhere else.

Moorgate
..Barbican
..Farringdon
..King's Cross St. Pancras
..Euston Square
..Great Portland Street
..Baker Street
..Edgware Road

One day I merely look at Paddington underground sign through the window and stay on: Bayswater, Notting Hill Gate, High Street Kensington… Sloane square…Embankment…Aldgate, and get on the next train back from Liverpool Street.

22nd June. I use the shelter to keep out of the sun which surrounds me like something unbearable. A man swigs from a can of coke. The large woman he's with shifts her weight from foot to foot very slowly.

We board and I sit away from them. We pass a house with a huge lawn being mown by a man on a garden tractor. If it were me I'd go up and down thinking of my father.

28th June. I sit on the right but face the wrong way, so it feels as if I'm on the left. By the time I recognise what's coming over my shoulder its details are diminishing and it frustrates me. I want to see it coming, getting bigger and bigger before it zooms past, a feature on the map coming to me and, if I don't move my head to follow it, whipping past my ear.

Perhaps it's each of the fifty years coming between me and that place where my father crashed. Fif-ty. Now I dream of journeys I make across country, emerging from a tunnel into a never-where. *It's like a glass wall, doctor. I can see the other side, but I keep bumping into it rather than passing through.*

Chapter Sixteen

I knocked on George's door. There was no reply so I went round the back of the house where I could hear noises down the garden. The door to the conservatory was open and there was a border spade propped against a wall. Then I saw George's head between some greenery. He stopped what he was doing when he saw me and waved.

He walked towards me with a fork in the crook of his arm just like my grandfather carried his gun. "Good to see you," he said, taking my hand in his, placing his other hand on top so that my hand was warmed by both of his. It went through me.

"You too."

"I'm keeping the place in order," he said. "Always something to be done. I haven't seen you around."

"I've been to Wales."

"You make it sound like a foreign country."

"It's a different world."

"Find what you're looking for?"

"I don't know what I'm looking for."

"Come on, we'll have a coffee," he said, pointing up the path to the house.

"So what's the problem?"

"I don't know. Mid-life crisis."

"War's a crisis. Everything else is just a stone in your shoe."

We sat in silence sipping the coffee. "I like this kitchen," I said, "it reminds me of my grandfather's."

"You should have run around in here."

There was a brief hiatus. "If someone had asked me what I'd be doing at fifty I wouldn't have said I'd be looking for my father."

"What would you have said?"

"I don't know."

"So what's the problem?"

"At ten I would have said pilot, twelve – draftsman, fourteen – vet, eighteen – teacher."

"You be*came* a teacher!"

"That's when my ambition was given concrete boots and thrown into a dock."

"You can't regret what you've spent your life doing."

"But you just said I should've been running around this kitchen."

"Regret isn't as big as you make it out to be."

"Perhaps it's the wrong word."

"Regret can't be allowed to mess you up."

"I must be messed up."

"You're just coming to terms with losing your mother."

"Have you come to terms with it?"

"No."

"I feel as if I've escaped one prison to find myself in another."

"Your mother was a good woman."

"She deceived me."

"It was her way of coping."

"I'm not coping now."

"Yes you are. You're just looking for direction."

"I'm looking for my father."

"Same thing. You need to find him, then you can move on. Then you'll have direction."

"I'm retiring."

"When did you decide that?"

"Oh, I've been thinking about it."

"At fifty?"

"I don't *need* to work. I've never done anything with my salary. I've just saved and saved. Besides, I've done my bit."

"Can you *do* that?"

"Yes."

"What will you *do*?"

"Don't know. Go to America."

"Find your father, then decide what to do."

"You were my father, really."

"Never. Your mother was adamant. I would do anything for her. It was all on her terms. It's a shame you never had a father but I have never regretted not being your father."

"Did my mother talk about my father?"

"Never."

"She never talked to *me* about him. When I asked she just blocked it. I found out more about him from what was in the box."

Shotguns are beautiful. My grandfather taught me that. It was a tool first, which protected the game he looked after. Then it provided food for the table, which is what he preferred. He was a good shot, too, or at least, that's what I thought as a boy.

He gave me a .410 first, a Webley and Scott bolt action, just right for me. I loved the weight of the cartridge in my hand before I slotted it into the chamber, the stepped knurl of the bolt, and its kick. My grandfather's gun was a side-by-side boxlock. He called it his work gun, that he carried with him when he was checking the pheasants and keeping down the vermin which he hung from a fence or convenient branch.

When I shot my first crow I shouted, *I got it! I got it!* and he admonished me.

"You've *killed* a crow. You've got to respect the crow. It's never a thing or a target. There is *grace* in what you've just done."

I didn't understand that at the time but knew it was important because Granddad was so earnest. When I didn't have my gun – I never went out unless I was with Granddad – I would see birds and animals and pretend to sight down the barrel of my gun and think, I could have killed it, whatever it was – at *that* moment.

"You are responsible for that animal's life at the instant you kill it," Granddad said. "You are the instrument – the gun is a part of you, not separate. Don't ever forget that. That crow was doing what you and me are doing. It was breathing and eating and drinking. It was *being* a crow. Now pick it up."

It was huge in my small hands, still alive, but I couldn't understand whether it was trying to hold on to something or trying to let go. "It's warm," I said.

"See?"

The crow became heavier in my hand.

"There," Granddad said, "he's gone now."

I filled up, aware of the gravity of the crow in my hand. It wasn't being a crow any more, with the strength and cockiness and presence it possessed minutes before. The joy of having killed the crow and the realisation about what I had done twisted in my chest.

These things come back to me now as I put my grandfather's gun together: lock and stock, fore-end and barrels.

"Craftsmanship, even in run-of-the-mill guns," Granddad said. "Look." The lock and the stock fitted perfectly. "Engineering and woodwork."

I brought the gun up to my shoulder and sighted down the barrel to the pin at the end. It was too short for me; I probably couldn't hit a thing with it now. Thing. Sorry Granddad. Then I stood in front of the mirror and aimed at myself and made the sound a boy makes when he pretends to shoot a gun. Twice.

"And what did you find out?"

"I'm bigger than he was."

George smirked. "How did you work that out?"

"His uniform. His cap. Shoes. They were all in the box."

"Extraordinary," he said, taken aback, shaking his head. "He was practically *in* my barn."

"Yes."

"Anything else?"

"Photographs, wallet, medals, notebook."

George considered these. "What are the photos?"

"He and Mum. His crew. Someone showing off a trout."

"What about the notebook?"

"I can barely read it."

"What does that mean?"

"He reveals himself in ways beyond anything I could have hoped for."

"That's good though?"

"It hurts."

George looked down at the table top. "We're both hurt."

"But he's still not…*there*," I said, as if 'there' was a place I could find. "I need to keep on."

George looked at me then out the window. There was a long silence. "Well…" Another silence. That 'well' just drifted off into nothing. "I'd like to see the photos."

"Of course."

"There was nothing else?"

"My grandfather's gun too."

"I liked *him*," George said. "When you went out with him it was sometimes an opportunity for your mother and I to spend time together." He looked at me guiltily.

"It's okay," I said. "I don't blame you. Pointless. My mother seemed to have a spell over both of us."

"I don't think she was as cunning as that. I think she was just locked up in something."

"How does that make you feel now? Do you really think she loved you?"

There was a long pause. "Yes." A pause. "No." Another pause. "Yes." Pause. "I don't know," he said quietly, shaking his head, looking out of the window. "What are you going to do with the gun?"

"Haven't thought about it."

"Always something to shoot here, if you like."

"Gun's too small for me."

"Well, the offer's there. Just come round."

I took the gun out of the bag and put it on the counter. "My grandfather's," I said. "It's too small for me."

"Let's have a look," he said. He put it together. "Haven't seen one of these for a while," he said, looking through the barrels. "Bores look fine. Right, two choices: we can make a new stock for it, which, frankly, will be expensive and isn't worth it for a modest weapon such as this, or, you can buy an extension pad which, in comparison, is a few pounds."

"Really?"

"If you want it fitted to you, properly, with the comb and the length and the sightline, it's an investment on an investment gun, which this isn't, but if you're just doing a bit of rough shooting, a pad will do the job. And you'll be able to use it straight away."

"Pad it is then."

He had several leather pads which just slotted on to the stock. He sized me up and slotted one on, slapping it into position with the ball of his hand. "There you go, try that." I raised it to my shoulder and sighted down to the bead. He had me sight down the barrel to his eye. "I'd say that was good. How does it feel?"

"Much better."

Chapter Seventeen

I know that the world is flat when I stand on top of the control tower. The horizon is a tree-line or a cluster of roofs. There are no hills but for the huge white hills which drift in the blue above. Deep wheat encircles the tower as if it stands on an island awash. Parallel lines show where the tractors have been; parallel lines show where the aeroplanes have been. I scan the horizon and wonder from which direction my father would have returned.

...bringing her in alone. The guns were jettisoned over the channel and he ordered the crew to bail out. There's one prop turning slowly and the engine is trailing smoke all over Suffolk, the undercarriage won't come down and there's a bomb in the bay. He's going to set her down on her belly. The fire crews are ready. The Fort is full of holes. The tail fin has a hole the size of a football, the rudder's sticking and it's taking all of his strength to keep her up long enough to clear the trees. The flat wide field is a bed on which to flop. The whole field holds its breath. The tower rails are gripped. His wrists and elbows and shoulders are braced as he lets her down a feather at a time. Adjusting with his feet, his eyes on the runway, he's going to set her down so gently that she'll think she's still in the air. He doesn't want to upset her or he'll be blown to each corner of the triangle. He has the weight of the flying gear over his shoulders. Her tubes and lines and rivets are aching to stop. He's aware of the dirt under his nails, a buzzing in his ears, his sweating head, the balls of his feet. He sets her down, the props buckle, the belly gun crunches against the runway, bits of her break off and the sound of all that metal gouging into the grass as she slews around twists in the guts of those watching...

The wheat tick-tick-ticks in the breeze.

Now it's all farmland. Then it was a massive clearing with three runways: one of 6,337 feet and two of 4,400 feet. I wonder what it would have looked like to the crews as they returned from a mission. More than a huge triangle. A wind blows across Suffolk and ruffles my thin hair. The clouds are low and there is a sky vast above them where my father flew. He's on a cloud looking down on me. *Hi Son.*

The tower is full of holes now. There are no doors or windows and the walls are pocked where the Americans shot it up when they left. The ground floor is strewn with fifty years of being open to the elements. There are owl pellets in a room on the first floor. There's no glass in the 'eye' on the roof. It's an empty landlocked lighthouse. There was an ordnance building, motor pool, photo lab, bomb aiming training, gunnery instruction, briefing rooms, parachute packing, radar, chapel, cinema, gymnasium, Nissen huts, fuel dumps, mess hall, sports field, operations block. Most of it gone by the time I shot the woods and fields and hedges around it.

I look over to George's place, the very tops of the trees of his woods peeking above the skyline.

My father flew complex machines; I wrote on a blackboard with a piece of chalk. He commanded a group of men who were highly trained: navigator, bombardier, gunners; I commanded a group of teachers who were highly trained at moaning even though nobody died. He dropped bombs; I studied history. He married my mother; I am still married to her.

"I haven't lived."

"I don't know what you mean," George said.

"Lived. I mean *lived*. My father *actually* lived. He felt everything."

"What your father did was extraordinary."

"I'm envious."

"There's nothing to be envious of. He died. Thousands died."

"My life has been easy and empty."

"Your life has been different."

"My father fought and loved and died. He did something worthwhile. He had a reason. I've flown desks in warm rooms."

"Look, what you're going through is something you should've come to terms with years ago. Losing your mother has brought this about. Teaching is a noble profession."

"I did it because of my mother. It was *all* for her."

"Everything I did was for her, too. That's what we did."

"You chose to do so. I didn't."

"Yes you did. You've had the privilege of a university education which you couldn't have enjoyed were it not for your father, and you've shaped the futures of thousands of children. Think of that. *That* is extraordinary. You're a part of what goes on, not all of it."

I looked out of the window across the field. "Yes, I'm sorry."

"What are you going to do with yourself in your retirement?"

"One thing at a time."

"The first thing?"

"I don't know, I don't know."

Chapter Eighteen

It was dumb to turn up at George's and shoot without any preparation, but Granddad had merely thrown swedes for me to practise.

"When it goes straight up, bring the bead up from below, touch the edge then pull the trigger. When it comes straight across you from left or right, bring the bead right through it to the far edge and pull the trigger, continuing to swing through or you'll miss behind."

Bits of swede broke off. It was like getting my own back after all the times I'd been made to eat them. They were much easier to hit, too, than the birds and animals which never behaved like swedes when they appeared.

"I used to do what I call the circuit," George said. "If you walk back up the drive and take the path to the right after the gate, that'll take you through the wood. Just follow the track. It may be a little overgrown, so watch your step. Then when you come out of the wood, you'll come out down there," he said, pointing. "Then you can take a stroll through the fields. There are five in all. You can't get lost because you're always in sight of the house. I never went into the last field because it's too close to the lane, just in case. Come in when you're done. I'm not going anywhere."

I went back down the drive with the gun open in the crook of my arm. I took two cartridges out of Granddad's belt, dropped them in and closed the gun, rested my thumb on the safety catch and stepped forward slowly and quietly. The leaves were beginning to turn. The path ran alongside a fence with an open field on the left and the dense wood on the right. I could see woodpigeons in the distance. Then where the fence met another, the path went right into the wood, a mix of oak and beech and sycamore.

I heard jays and magpies and crows but saw nothing.

Then I heard a crow ahead. As I got closer I realised it was high in the canopy. I looked and looked but couldn't see it, then it broke off and I lifted the gun and fired and missed. I sagged. It was just a miss. There *would* be misses. But the effect was beyond a mere miss.

I took out the spent cartridge and slipped it onto my middle finger as I slipped another into the gun. That's what Granddad used to do! When I was small he had entertained me with finger puppets made out of empty cartridges. 12 bore for adults, .410 for children. He painted them: the butcher, the baker, the candlestick maker. Cartridges as finger puppets! Full – death, empty – fun.

I don't know why I thought I could just go out and start shooting as I did with my grandfather. I was different. I don't think I'd held a gun since my early twenties. I was different in mind and body. About three stones heavier. I don't know how my mind had changed in that time. It was history. There'd been a revolution. Its map had been redrawn. Boundaries had moved. Even north was in a different place.

I had discharged only one barrel. I had thought about the second barrel but in the time it took me to do so I had missed the opportunity to shoot. I had to think about putting my finger on the second trigger, behind the first. When I was younger I hadn't had to think. It would have been one – miss, two. Today it had been one – miss, what do I do now?

When my father had flown over occupied Europe there were Germans beneath him who tried to knock him out of the sky with big guns. Different guns. But they were still guns. Perhaps there was a German grandfather and his grandson, too, trying to knock my father out of the sky in 1943. *Sie können turbulenzen wahrend des fluges erleben*: You may experience turbulence in flight.

Then I broke through the glass.

Dyfed-Powys Constabulary
CRICKHOWELL
18th September 1973

Sir,

I received information of a break-in at Llanbedr Church which occurred on the night of the 16th-17th September.

Mrs. Henrietta Burgoyne, Churchwarden.

"I had not realised that the church had been broken into until I went to sweep the floor around the altar. My first impression was that someone had left a baby swaddled on the floor. Then I saw that it was a pile of stones which had looked like a child in the poor light.

The stones had been arranged as a cairn. There were nine stones.

I looked around the rest of the church but could find nothing out of place or anything missing. I do not know why someone would leave a pile of stones in front of the altar."

This being the statement of Mrs. Henrietta Burgoyne, taken by me,

Gareth John
Police Constable 822

Dyfed-Powys Constabulary
CRICKHOWELL
11th November 1973

Sir,

    I attended a disturbance at the Red Dragon Public House, Llanbedr 11th November.

    When I arrived the publican, Mr. Roger Rees, had gained control of the situation. I took his statement:

    "Mr. Glyn Williams, of Nant Farm, took umbrage at something Mr. Hugh Burgoyne of Ty Mawr had said about America's contribution in World War Two. Mr. Williams said that Mr. Burgoyne did not know what he was talking about. Mr. Burgoyne said he knew more than 'a stupid drunk'. Mr. Williams said that he did not wish to stay in such disagreeable company. He purchased a bottle of beer to take out. As he passed Mr. Burgoyne he struck him on the head with the bottle which caused the laceration.

    In my opinion, Mr. Burgoyne behaved in a provocative manner and Mr. Williams should not have struck Mr. Burgoyne. I have banned both customers until such time that they apologise to me."

    I interviewed Mr. Williams the following day. His statement:

    "I was very upset by what Mr. Burgoyne said. I know what Americans gave in the War. But I am sorry for my actions and the trouble I have caused."

    I interviewed Mr. Burgoyne also. His statement:

    "It was my fault. I had too much to drink and I should not have said what I said. I do not wish to press charges against Mr. Williams."

The matter is closed.
Gareth John
Constable

REPORT INTO THE HILL FIRES

September 1983

The incidents:

1. *****
2. +++++
3. *****

The latter was so extensive that it required crews from Brecon and Abergavenny to attend also.

As a result, Commander John Wallis of Crickhowell Fire Brigade requested that we investigate. Commander Wallis believes that all indications are that the fires were started deliberately. There is concern that such fires could pose a risk to life and property. Commander Wallis believed that police presence would help deter the person(s) responsible from carrying out any more attacks.

I spent two weeks on vehicular and walking patrols in those areas identified as being at risk. Commander Wallis took me to the fire beds and demonstrated that the fires could not have started naturally.

When we approached Pen Twyn Mawr on foot we saw a tall white-haired man who stopped when he saw us and went back the way he came. We attempted to catch up with him. He disappeared from view over the side of the hill and when we reached that spot we could see no sign of him. We searched the area but could not account for the man's disappearance, there being open hillside only and no cover.

Retracing our route back to the force Landrover, we came upon a cross made from scrap metal.

No more fires have been reported.

Gareth John
Insp. Investigating Officer

(Appended Sheet)

I have been able to establish that the metal cross found on the patrol of 18th September marks the crash site of an American aircraft from 1943. This was initially investigated by my father, Sergeant Arthur John (retired). He said that he and Mr. Glyn Williams of Nant Farm (deceased) had erected the cross from pieces of wreckage in memory of the crew who all perished.

Gareth John
(Investigating Officer)

Chapter Nineteen

I was already at the table in the window when she came in with a plate in each hand. She stopped, looked at me with a puzzled expression, then smiled. I didn't expect that. Then she went about her business. By the time I registered what she had done, the smile with which I responded was too late, so I was keen for her to see me smile when she came back through.

I ordered food at the bar and she brushed past with more plates. It seemed that I wouldn't get to talk to her because someone else was waiting my table, but then she appeared with my basket of bread.

"I didn't expect to see you again," she said. "You disappeared."

"Yes, I did, didn't I?"

"You did," she said, in a gently admonishing tone.

"I had to go."

"How long are you here for?"

"I'm booked in a few nights. See how it goes." She maintained eye contact the whole time.

"See you later."

"I'd like that."

I have spent time looking at her. Just looking. She wears a V-neck which exposes a large area of her chest. 'Area' is the wrong word. So is 'expanse', which is the next word which comes to mind. It's so very lovely. *So* very. How can I emphasise it without 'so' and 'very'? I don't know a word which can describe its qualities, or rather, the influence its qualities have upon me. 'Influence', too, is wrong. Whatever qualities – whatever that skin is – it does something to me. I have lingered on the slopes of each breast. I have wanted to touch them, feel their particular smoothness and shape in my hands. I have wanted my hands to be their bra cups. I have wanted them against my face. I can close my eyes and feel their softness. Would they be warm? Then I look at her neck. Its musculature makes me want to bite and kiss and lick it. Then her mouth. She smiles. I am conscious of *not* smiling. Perhaps she sees a man who nods and listens, interested in what she has to say. Perhaps she is bored by me, a poor match for her animated self. She's vibrant. Her teeth are big and white. I like their sheen. I want to run my tongue over them. I feel her lips cushion mine. She bites my lips. My hand takes her head and keeps her there, kissing me, her hair falling forward because I'm on my back and she's sitting on me, and I can lose myself in the waterfall of her hair. And now she stops kissing my mouth and kisses my left cheek and I kiss the left side of her face and it's the same smoothness as her chest. She leans forwards so that she presents a nipple to my mouth and I take it gently and play my lips and tongue around it. Oh how I love this. I am going to remember it forever and ever, Amen. This must be what it's like to fly. *Dad, is this as good as flying?* I sit opposite a woman, looking at her. I want sex with her. I've been nodding and haven't heard a word she's said. I disappeared. I went to a place men go when they want sex with a woman and they're on automatic pilot as the woman talks about, well, whatever. I am looking at her from my place on the shelf where day by day dust settles on me like a soft blanket under which I've been sleeping for years. I can't remember the last time I had sex. It must have been Sylvia. I wonder what *she's* doing now.

My mother was the blanket to which I clung. Right? I've been fooling myself. Rather than not wanting to upset her I've merely found it easier not to engage with the world around me. Not having a life other than the one which orbited my mother, meant that I had nothing at all to distract me from my career. That brings to mind some high-powered job, though – I don't know what, exactly – but not education. For me that's just been crowd control, avoiding people's toes and smiling. Inanely, probably. It all came so naturally to me. That's what living with mum did for me. And now that it's gone I have to deal with the world I haven't had to take part in before. I am a fifty year old man growing up. I make models of aeroplanes my father flew and fought against. My father is plastic and I dream about sitting next to him in the co-pilot's seat. I make the noise of an aeroplane with my lips pursed like a trombonist's embouchure and the look on her face makes me realise what I have just done.

"I thought you'd found your father and gone."

"No. I couldn't last time."

"So what's taken you so long?"

"I crashed my car. Then I couldn't get here."

"There's always the train."

"That's how I came."

"You haven't got a car then."

"No."

"So how are you going to find your father?"

"I'll walk."

"Not from here. It's too far."

"Is it? Taxi then."

"Don't be daft! What are you going tell the driver, 'Take me to where my father crashed his plane in the war'?" We laughed at the absurdity. "Besides," she continued, "you're not going up a hill in those," pointing to my boat shoes.

"It's all I've got."

"They're okay for mooching about but you can't go up a hill in them. Haven't you got any boots?"

"Never done any walking."

"It's not about walking, it's about not breaking your neck. Pop in the hiking shop on the High Street, you'll get something there. Good too, they've got an end-of-line corner. You never know. But you can't go anywhere in those. This ain't Suffolk. And you can borrow my car."

I have never seen a raven in Suffolk. I've seen them at the Tower in London but they're not like this. Here they are majestic. This one flaps off what's left of a rabbit on the lane and floats out over the valley. *Kraank-kraank-kraank*: a crag in flight.

It's dark even though it's meant to be the middle of the day. The hills make me feel small. The further I go up this lane the more it feels that I am going into something I don't understand. The hill rises on my left and falls away on my right into the valley before it rises again opposite. Then all I can see is the way ahead with hedges high on either side and a hill in front. There isn't enough room for the sky. The hedges become higher and the lane narrower. The trees are close to the fence, tall and impenetrable. I can see the ground sloping away in the gaps between their trunks. Dandelions brighten the banks, white-beaconed seed-heads globe against the green. Daisies prink around them. Everything funnels me forward. Perhaps there will be a passage between two rocks through which I'll emerge into that other world where my father is, his Shangri-La. He'll still be twenty-two. *Welcome*, he'll say, *I knew you'd come one day*. Then there's a fiddler's-elbow bend, the lane curving round the contour of the next hill and looking back from where I've just come, an open view. Then another fiddler's bend around which the lane becomes a track and runs to the end of the valley. It stops at a gate behind which there is a sign nailed to a tree – NO ACCESS – and darkness I don't associate with daytime.

I'm crawling along the lane with the wipers on and can't remember the first spots of rain which made me turn them on. It's light rain, enough to blur the hills. Next time I'll bring the map with me. The rain strengthens. The wipers can't clear it quickly enough and I have to put them on double speed. Still the wipers can't cope. I haven't known rain like this pelting the glass and the roof of the car. The car is a chamber of sound, a rain chamber, reverberating. I can't see the road ahead even when I slow down. I nearly go through a hedge then pull in to a gateway. The car is rocking and there is a sudden downpour when the rain intensifies. If the rain was hail the car would be damaged. If the rain were bullets I'd be dead.

I don't know where I go next, clearly somewhere I'm not conscious of having existed. That's the only way I can explain it. I return to a sound I recognise. It's the drunk at the door again. I'll tell him where to go this time.

Light hurts my eyes and I can't see. Knocking. Go away! I can hear him but my eyes haven't adjusted.

"Sir," the voice says.

I am in a half-asleep, half-awake place. I become aware of a blue budgie flocking about me.

"Sir, you can't park here." A face against the window. Light in my eyes. Sir. "Sir!" A peaked cap. A face against the window. "You have to move. You all right, Sir?"

I make sense of it all in a moment. A police officer. I wind down the window.

"You can't park here. You're blocking the lane."

"No, of course not, sorry." I start the car and pull away a little faster than I had intended, the budgie in the car disappearing the instant I go round the next bend.

Back at the hotel I spread out the map and retrace where I've been. I mis-read the bends. I had driven right past the turn off for the crash site. I might even have looked right at it without knowing. I hadn't wanted to go there in the rain anyway. I wanted to be able to see what I was looking at. I want it to be clear. *I* want to be clear.

"The forecast is hot tomorrow. You sure you want to go to the crash site? Wait till the weekend when it'll be cooler."

"I've got a hat," I said, as if that would protect me.

"A hat?" She laughed. "You can't drink a hat."

"I don't get you."

"Your father can wait a little longer, a couple of days at least. Listen, you need to relax."

"Relax."

A pause. "Can you swim?"

"You think I should go swimming?"

"It'll help you relax."

"I can't remember the last time I went swimming."

"You don't have to."

"I haven't got my trunks."

"You're showing your age now."

"Eh?"

"Trunks. Not heard that for a while. You can get some in Aber. Then I'll take you to a pool."

We left it at that. I started to think of her in a swimming costume. I knew what I would look like: overweight and hairy. I never seemed to be exposed to anything these days, though I was always outdoors as a child. You've got the sun in you, Granddad would say. What would she *look* like? I had seen her in a thin skirt, the light penetrating it to define the shape of her thighs, her calf dusted with a faint tan. I was stirred by that smooth triangle of chest a little darker than her legs, the definition in her neck I wanted to taste.

Chapter Twenty

I had been looking at my knees in the bathroom mirror only the night before so enjoyed the sight of her knees below the line of her skirt when I sat next to her in the car. The knuckles of the joints were definite and shapely, a hollow at each side somewhere I wanted to put my tongue. I had not experienced such want before. There was some little aspect of her that became new to me each time I looked at her, the smooth pear of her calf, the mallow of her lips.

We approached the spot along the path next to the river. At first I took the sound for wind soughing through the trees but there was no wind and the sound came from the rapids intermittently spaced down the course of the river as it swept past us. The path was damp and slippery with moss on the stones and puddles where the recent rain was untouched by the sun. Beech and sycamore saplings grew out of unlikely places in the dry-stone wall on our left. The stones which layered the path had been worn into uneven steps amongst roots tangled round them. She came to a stop.

"Listen," she said, "there's water there–" pointing to the river – "and there's water there–" pointing to the water trickling out of the wall. "Water meets water." She smiled at me. She walked on again and I concentrated on my footing as my shoes slipped on the stones. The vegetation thinned where large flat-topped rocks created a natural platform. She set down her bag and blanket and cushion. She put her hands on her waist and shook her head. "You can't beat this. I've been coming here ever since I can remember."

A green harmony of trees clustered on the opposite bank. Here the river was broad and deep.

"You can swim from there to there," she said, indicating the two points at the top and bottom of the pool, about fifty yards long. "You can get out over there where there's a shelf."

"This isn't what I expected when you said we were going for a swim."

"This is better than any *pool*."

The water was green and dark. The rocks gradually lost themselves in its depths. A steady run of small rafts of foam ran the river's currents.

"It looks quite fast," I said.

"It's fine. And I don't think you'll be troubled by sharks today."

I looked down at my new swimming shorts with their bold shark print. Now I felt self-conscious. "It was all they had in the shop."

"Really?"

"Only thing in my size, I mean."

"Nothing else at all?"

"I didn't think a bikini was suitable."

"Good decision."

I tried to be nonchalant as she slipped out of her skirt and unbuttoned her linen shirt. She was whole in front of me. I wanted to touch her and feel her smoothness against me. "You going in?" I said.

"That's why we came." She stepped out onto the rock shaped like an animal's back, her toes clamping the surface. Then she dived. She surfaced with a whoop. "Come on!"

I looked downstream to the stone bridge arching across the river then back to her. I dived into the green blur where light spangled around me. I wanted to stay down but the river brought me to the surface.

"That better?"

"Wonderful."

"Told you."

"It's magic."

"Yes, it's magic."

I swam to her as she stepped onto the shelf of rock along the opposite bank. She glistened in the sun. I stepped out next to her. She had her hands on her waist again, looking up and down the river. A raven *kraanked* overhead, its call muffled by the sound of the water. She walked upstream a few yards then dived and I saw the light stripe her beneath the surface. I dived, then, consciously trying to stay under, to make out what was about me, but the river held me up again. She sat on the rock from which she had entered the water and I joined her. Her thigh and shoulder touched mine and she kept them against me. I wanted to taste the water that beaded between her breasts.

"It's not the most comfortable rock," I said.

"Get back in then."

I eased myself into the river and trod water as I faced her. It was good to be in the water and looking at her. She smiled at me. I loved her against the green play of the trees. Then I went back to the rock and noticed her small foot next to my hand. "Have you ever been in an aeroplane?"

She dropped her jaw and looked at me sternly from beneath her brow. "What kind of a question's that?"

"It's a have-you-ever-been-in-an-aeroplane kind of question."

"Of course I have!"

"You'd be surprised who would say no to that."

"Oh, I see. *You* haven't."

"As a matter of fact, no."

"That's crazy."

"What's crazy is that my father died on a hill *here*."

"Everyone's been in an aeroplane these days."

"I've never had reason to."

"Not even for a holiday?"

"I don't do holidays."

"What, never?"

"My mother always took me to her cousin's in London. I went to Ostende once. School trip."

"So you *have* been on holiday."

"It never felt like a holiday." There was another silence. "You know, some people have never been on a train let alone an aeroplane."

"Now I *know* you've been on a train."

"I like trains."

"I've decided that you need a holiday and you've got to fly. Book a holiday."

"I dream about flying with my father."

"That's nice."

"'Nice'."

"You know, I mean good."

"I don't know how."

"You're connected. You're together."

"He was always on the mantelpiece when I was a boy. He only ever flew in my dreams."

"I'll join you for my break."

"Don't they mind you fraternising with guests?" I said.

"You make it sound like a crime."

"Sorry, I mean just talking."

"There's no 'just' about it."

"No."

"Something's happening."

"Yes."

"Something you and I haven't got time to be silly about. I haven't got time to be silly."

"No."

"Stop saying 'no'."

"I'm sorry. I don't know what to say."

"Oh come on, don't let me down."

"I'm not letting you down, I'm trying."

"Perhaps you're trying too hard. Don't try, don't think about it."

"Okay."

"You're doing it again, you're thinking."

 I don't reply.

"Stop it."

"What do you want me to do?"

"I want us to go to your room."

"Okay."

"No it's not 'okay'. I want something and I think you can give it to me."

"What does that mean?"

"It came out wrong. It's not like that. I want…" She looked at me for a long time, puzzled. She ran her fingers around the rim of her coffee cup. "I'm sorry." She stood up and walked out towards the kitchen. I thought she'd gone to fetch something but as time wore on the bar emptied and she didn't come back.

In a hotel in a strange place I am trying to find a way to my father. There is a woman who makes me feel inadequate but I want to have sex with her. On the napkin I sketch a map of three spheres in which I write 'Mum', 'Dad' and 'Me', connecting them with lines I take to be a route between us.

Chapter Twenty-One

I sat in the garden across the road from the Bridgend Inn, its mixture of wooden and stone benches set back from the river bank by two cranked apple trees. The water was background music, the weir below the bridge taking it a step closer to the sea, a green water-colour wash which frothed and dissipated into a deep green pool where fallen apples bobbed against the bank.

I walked along the bridge. Each arch's span was bookended with a V-shaped niche where it was possible to sit. I looked down at the water running quickly and shallow over cobbled stones. Then I crossed the road. At once I saw a dipper flit from a stone to a step at the base of a low wall. It went down and up as if on an office chair, then dived into the clear water where I could see it 'flying'. It returned to the step when it surfaced and was joined by another, its back the colour of a gun barrel. The male. I watched them for a while, flitting away from this spot, taking it in turns to disappear and return. Then I went back to the pub garden and took the path downstream.

After a mile I stopped. Wide flat slabs of stone usually swept by water were exposed and dry; tall green grasses grew from fissures and there were hollows of stagnant water where flies fizzed. I went to where the rocks channelled the water, attracted by the sound and change of texture, the wide glide picking up momentum before rippling through and emerging in swirls the other side and gliding again.

The fast water constantly remade its shape and the sun flashed off it. In the slow water above, minute flashes of light sparked in the dark green background. I moved to the slack water where my shadow disturbed a trout eight inches long. It slipped under the ledge of the slab on which I stood before appearing again a couple of feet along, making for the open river. My grandfather would have liked to have caught that and put it back. "But not in the war," he'd have said, "we ate whatever we could get."

The sun went behind cloud and the whole scene became monochromatic. The absence of what had given the place grandeur caused me to concentrate on the weed floating in the slack water like rafts of something unpleasant. A moment before I would have been glad to be borne up by the currents. Now I didn't want to dip my foot. The grey wagtails in their yellow and grey tailcoats embodied the sun and the cloud as they flitted from rock to rock mid-stream.

On the bend ahead I saw a rod flicking line out onto the water and I made my way down the path towards it. As I got closer I was careful not to make a noise, careful where I trod. When I was close enough I stood up on the bank above the man fishing. He brought in his line and took the fly in his hand.

"Afternoon," he said, briefly looking up at me.

"I tried not to make a noise."

"You didn't. I saw you up on the bend."

"Any luck?"

"You mean joy. No joy. Not yet."

"What works here?"

"You fish?"

"My grandfather used to take me as a boy."

"Depends. But you can't beat a pheasant tailed nymph."

"Travelling light I see."

"A rod, reel, box of flies, that's all you want. All the other stuff's for daft buggers."

I laughed. He didn't take his eye from each cast he made, each retrieve, winding the line with his left hand in a practised sleight of hand. He never looked at where his line went behind him as he cast. Back and out, back and out, describing beautiful shapes in the air from the past to the future of the moment in hand. Upstream and drift down.

I sat on the bank and watched his hand tick-tock the rod so that the line ran out through the rings smoothly and the fly fell on the water oh-so-lightly, a speck on a thread of gossamer.

He flicked the rod and it arced to a fish which ratcheted line from the reel. The fish took off to an overhang but he managed to bring it back into the swim and a couple of minutes later, after it had made another break, he led its nose into the net.

"A good two pounder. Want a look?" He unhooked the fly and held the brown trout in his hands and lifted it up as if it were a gift. The golden dappled flank sparkled in his hands. "Look at that."

Its big mouth looked hungry to live, its fins made it look like an aeroplane for the sub-aquatic world, gliding between the rocks and the currents' turbulence.

"I've put two back but this one's a plate fish." He held it down on the grass with one hand and used a priest to kill it with one blow.

"So what's *your* obsession?"

"What?"

"Rugby? Football? Cricket? The 'gee-gees', as my dad calls them?" she said.

"No."

"Must be something."

I struggled for something not to disappoint her. "I make models." She didn't react. "Airfix models," I said, to clarify.

"The little plastic man," she said.

"Yes."

"Do you usually carry the bits around with you?"

"My father."

"Ah yes, I remember. That little plastic man's not going to explain anything to you."

"It's not just the man, it's the whole kit. It's from the aeroplane he flew."

"I don't know what you're on about."

"Well, there were airfields all over Suffolk. Most of the kids I went to school with had some connection with the airmen. Some of the village women ended up in the States."

"Why didn't you?"

"My father died in 1943 so there was no need for my mother to go anywhere."

"Ever met his family?"

"No."

"Shame."

"My mother never had anything to do with his family. He died, we didn't go, that's it."

"But surely you wanted to know about his family."

"It wasn't like that. My father was unique. Everything started and ended with him. He was a self-contained world."

I looked up at the aeroplanes scoring the blue sky's ice. They were so high up that I could just make out their shape, their wings and fuselage. I wondered from where they had taken off: Heathrow? Paris? Berlin? They were heading west. In a few minutes they would be over the west Wales coast over the Irish Sea, then Eire and then the wide Atlantic.

Through my binoculars I could see the way the engines' exhausts – that's what they looked like – began some distance behind the wings, twisting into the ribbon which described where they'd sucked in and thrust out the air. They chopped and chopped and the passengers relaxed with gin or wine. At least, that's what James Bond films had me believe.

All those people up there were unaware that I was watching their progress. *Where*? What *did* those people do which meant they had to fly?

I had heard of near misses, incidents when two aeroplanes came too close to each other. Looking at them I thought they were close. Perhaps they were at different heights. It was hard to tell. They criss-crossed so that they marked an event: an X. It was soon unmade, though, as the trails spread and widened. There were three aeroplanes up there going in the same direction.

When I turned left up the road into the hills there was a single cloud as fine and light as a swan's feather in an intense, blue sky. It looked unreal. Then as I climbed into the hills and the road narrowed into a single track with passing spaces, the clouds gathered as if on cue. They came to nothing, though, moving north-east sedately, their shadows moving across the hills beneath them. One moment sheep were grey, the next they were startlingly white in green fields. I could just remember the way to where I had ended up in the torrential rain on the previous occasion, but now everything was beautiful.

I reached the dog-leg bend and pulled in at the entrance to Cwm Farm where an oak with a huge girth stood just inside the gate. From here there was an unobstructed view of the hill where my father had crashed.

A post van sped through Cwm Farm gate and down the drive. I was looking up at the hill as other hills formed a 'V' in front of it. Cloud shadows moved across it slowly. There were a few sheep and half a dozen small bushes scattered on its slopes. It reminded me of photographs of Everest in the newspaper as it squeezed from behind the hills immediately in front of it. But this was gentle with forestry and lush hill grass in the foreground.

I looked through my binoculars. There was a figure silhouetted on the skyline.

"Can I help you?" I turned to see a postman hanging out of his van window. I recognised him. The drunk in the suit from the hotel.

"I'm fine, thanks."

"You look as if you're lost."

"No. I'm okay. Thanks anyway."

"You have to be careful round here." He nodded, slipped the van into gear and wheel-spun away.

I looked through the binoculars again and the figure on the skyline had gone. A large silhouetted bird flew into the binoculars' field of view. I waited until I saw its diamond-shaped tail: raven. The sound of water running down the valley, Grwyne Fechan, separated me from the peak in the near distance.

Chapter Twenty-Two

"It's easy if they're coming straight at you," Granddad said. "You don't have to worry about swinging through the bird, you just keep the bead on it and pull the trigger. If you miss it's because you're not lined up properly."

I had been watching woodpigeons flying across the field and thinking I should position myself somewhere along their flight line. Better still, I should set up a hide and put out some decoys and pick them off as they came to the pattern. I had neither a hide nor decoys.

My gun was broken in the crook of my arm and I watched as yet another couple of birds took the flight line across the field in the distance. But these jinked and turned towards me. They kept coming. I closed the gun, thumbed the safety catch forward and waited. They came on, I shouldered Granddad's gun, beaded the left bird, pulled the trigger, beaded the second, pulled the second trigger. They crumpled, feathers separated, wings looked as if whatever connected them to the body was shut off and they folded towards the ground. The birds hit the earth with a bump, the first dead, the second flapping. One shot each.

"I didn't imagine the shots, then. I see you've had more luck today," George said as I came into the garden from the field.

"A right and a left. Pure luck. Came straight on."

"Ah well, don't knock luck. It's that certain indefinable something that brings great relief. Shall we have those for lunch?"

I looked down at the birds in my hand, their necks between my fingers, their weight pulling towards the ground. I held them up to look at them. "Why not?"

George plucked them on the kitchen table and passed them to me to take the meat off the bone. The breasts were patterned with dark bloody holes where the pellets had gone through. I introduced the nose of the blade and worked either side of the sternum to separate flesh from bone. George watched me. I put the first breast on the board in front of him.

"I've never seen it done like that."

"My grandfather. And mother. She could have skinned a flea."

"She skinned me."

I laughed. I fried the breasts with onions and George cut thick slices of bread and buttered them.

"They look good," he added, when we sat down to eat them.

"You know, when I used to shoot with my grandfather, it wasn't easy to kill a bird. No. That's not right. It was easy to kill them, having the opportunity was difficult. It was as if these two were going to be killed, whatever."

"It's just like anything else. We're not in control. In the War people learned that quickly and you were reminded again and again."

"This might sound strange, but I envy you the War."

"You're right, it is strange."

"But people lived."

"You've said."

"They did. I'm fifty. I haven't."

"Well do something about it."

"It's too late."

"You live in the moment. This is a moment. We're enjoying it. We eat the pigeon, we talk. We live. You be aware of the moment. Now. That's what living is. Being grateful."

"I'm beginning to realise that."

"So, it's never too late."

"I've met a woman."

"Good."

"She lives where my father crashed."

"Do you love her?"

"No, I don't think so."

"Either you do or you don't."

"It's not that easy."

"Yes it is! Love is black and white."

"That's the Law."

"It's love, too."

"Is that how it was with you and my mother?"

"Certainly."

"I don't understand it."

George looked straight at me, lifted his eyebrows and ran his hand down over his nose and mouth. "That," he said, pointing at his plate, "was good."

Chapter Twenty-Three

"Come on, you're walking me home," she said as she pushed out through the doors.

I followed. "Is it far?"

"Nothing's far. Anyway, would it matter?"

"I didn't mean anything by it."

"I know."

We crossed the road and went down High Street. As we rounded the bend at the top of Bridge Street, what swept away from me was a street similar to something I'd seen on the TV. "It's like the Hovis advert," I said.

"I know."

"Did you know that street's actually in Shaftesbury in Dorset?"

"Is that so?" She raised her eyebrows.

"That's a useless piece of information, isn't it?"

She nodded. "Here we are, this is my Hovis house."

"You're teasing me."

"You started it."

"I'm sorry."

The door opened straight into the sitting room. A two-seater sofa, an easy chair, TV.

"Take a pew, I'll put the kettle on," she said as she went through to the kitchen. I sat on the sofa and took in the room. Fir cones arranged in height order on the mantelpiece. A boxy television. A seventies standard lamp with a large tasselled shade. A small table piled with books next to the easy chair.

The shelves either side of the chimney breast displayed skulls and pieces of wood. I went to them and examined the skulls in my hands.

"Sugar?" she called.

"No thanks." I heard the sound of a spoon rattling in a cup, then she appeared.

"You like my bones?" she said, handing me a cup.

"As a matter of fact, I do."

"Some people think I'm morbid."

"I can understand that."

"Do you think it's morbid?"

"No. I think they're beautiful."

"Really?"

"Really."

"Which is your favourite?"

"This one. I like birds."

"Know what it is?"

"A raven."

"I'm impressed. This one?"

"Fox."

"This one?"

"Sheep."

"You're good."

"My grandfather was a gamekeeper so I've seen almost everything in the country in various states of life and death: crows, rooks, jackdaws, jays, magpies, buzzards, kestrels, sparrowhawks, barn owls, tawny owls, little owls, badgers, stoats, weasels, rats and every kind of mouse. These make me feel at home. Did I just say that out loud?"

"You did."

"Now I sound strange."

She laughed. "Well, I wouldn't say they're comforting but I do find them beautiful. They're the most beautiful pieces of sculpture and they're all from around here."

"So what got you interested in skeletons?"

"I went fishing with my Dad when I was about eleven and we found a sheep's skull on the bank. This one. I loved the idea that this was what you couldn't see beneath the sheep and the notion of sheep and what a sheep meant to me. It all changed then. I thought there's a world beneath so many things, so much of what we see is superficial, and I wanted to know what. This sheep's skull has so many planes and orifices. It's a beautiful thing. It's not that it got me interested in skeletons per se, but got me interested in what a thing is. An object. An artefact. I wanted to make my own. Henry Moore was given an elephant's skull and he did lots of work from it."

"No elephants around here."

"Yes there are, white ones."

I laughed.

"No, not white elephants," she said. "Sheep."

"Of course! No tusks, though."

"Rams have horns and they're curlier. There are fewer, too, of course."

"I never thought there were elephants in Wales."

"It's an exotic place," she said earnestly. "I'm going upstairs now and in a little while I'm going to call you."

She kissed me and went through the open door in the corner of the room through which I could see a glow on the wall. I stayed on the sofa looking around the room then I got up and looked at the objects here. I picked up the raven's skull again. What was in it? The Black Mountains. And everything in them: the farms and lanes and hedges and trees and sheep and cows and horses and dogs and rocks and sun and wind and rain. Was that a raven I heard then? I listened. Movement upstairs muffled by the ceiling above me. She called.

The staircase rose between two walls so that it felt as if I was rising through a tunnel and the wooden stairs made sounds which registered my weight and tread.

"I'm in here," she said quietly.

Light glowed onto the landing from the open door on the left.

I'm looking out the cockpit at the Mustang flying alongside. The pilot glances across and waves. It's George. A jolt. The sky is cracked. I follow its uneven line to where it stops. A ceiling rose. I'm naked. Under a quilt.

There's a smell. It's a nice smell. I move my leg and touch something. It's warm and smooth. A leg. Her leg. Her smell. I'm safe.

The first thing I noticed in the bathroom was the skeleton of a trout in a box frame above the toilet, a filigree of precision. I peed. On the window sill was a salmon skull, its lower mandible jutting in a fierce statement of its presence. I washed my hands.

"I like the fish," I said, when I went back into the bedroom.

"My father gives them to me."

"The trout is so fine."

"It took me ages. There are a few bones missing I think."

"You framed it?"

"Of course." She sat up in bed, the quilt clamped over her breasts with her arms. "Stand there," she said, "I want to look at you."

Now I was aware of my nakedness. "I'm embarrassed," I said.

"You're lovely."

I looked down at my round belly, my white skin, my bent feet. "I don't see it," I said.

"We mustn't waste time. Do you know what I'm saying?"

"No."

"Promise me you will say when you do."

I was puzzled but I said, "I promise."

"Now come here." She giggled to herself. "It's so vulnerable now." She was looking at my penis. "It's a rare funghi." She put her mouth over it and squeezed it against the roof of her mouth with her tongue. "A rare taste, too. You haven't had much, er…"

"No."

"Incredible."

"You're embarrassing me."

"I don't mean to. But it is incredible."

"I suppose."

"There's no 'suppose'. Endearing, though."

"Doesn't feel endearing."

"I thought you were being gentlemanly."

140

"I am gentlemanly."

"I've never been loved like this."

"I see," I said, which was entirely empty of meaning as soon as I realised I'd said it. What did I see? If it meant that I understood, that was untrue.

"Look," she said, "I think there's something happening. You see it, don't you?"

Something was happening but I wasn't sure we were referring to the same thing.

"You're not a dud. You're the real thing. We can't waste our time." She added, "Where does your mother fit in?"

"She doesn't. Not anymore."

She looked puzzled, then said, "Good."

"History. No hobbies really. The usual stuff boys of my generation did. Stamps. Coins."

"Trainspotting?"

"No. Never got that."

"But you didn't carry on with stamps and coins into adulthood."

"You know anyone who did?"

"No. I never did those things."

"Do girls do stamps and coins?"

"None of my friends."

"Oh, I fished. Oh and shot, but I did those with my grandfather. He used to take me. We always did it together."

"But not anymore."

"Just been out with his gun, actually. First time in years. I only ever had time for history in between."

"What about your father's history?"

"Not the same. It was strictly a no-go. I never considered it. My mother's happiness was paramount. I was incredibly sensitive to it. The person she loved disappeared. One day he flew away and didn't come back. Then she had to watch him grow up: I look just like him."

"Yes, I can understand that it must have been difficult for her, but I just think it's odd that you're looking for him but not his family."

"Never occurred to me."

"You would've had grandparents and aunts and uncles and cousins."

"My mother used to say, *There was only your father*. He was all that mattered."

"That's all so wrong."

"That's what she wanted. *I loved your father*, she'd say, *not his family*. So, going to the States and meeting them wasn't going to change things. There was no point as far as she was concerned."

"But that wasn't fair on you."

"I didn't miss what I never had. My mother's parents were wonderful. One set of grandparents was fine for me."

Chapter Twenty-Four

"What the fuck!"

Her voice. She came into focus and out again.

"What the fuck!"

I was blinking and trying to see but my eyes were full of tears. My head hurt. I was sitting up and as things about me sharpened I could see blood. I was covered in blood. Her hands were cradling my head and she was looking into my face.

"Who was it?"

I was somewhere else. The back of my head hurt. When I moved it seemed as if my eyes had to catch up with where my head had gone, as if something was loose.

"Did you lose consciousness?"

"Yes," she said, answering for me.

"Did you?" the doctor asked again.

"I think so."

"You're not right, are you? I can see that." He shone a torch into my eyes. "We'll X-ray you to see if your head's okay but clearly your nose will need manipulating."

There'd been a knock on the door. "You get that," she said. There was an instant between opening the door and recognising the person who had knocked before I saw the fist coming from a long way away to my nose. I saw it like a cartoon's slow motion, bigger and bigger and bigger until the knuckles, ridged like hills, went out of focus at that spot in my vision where it was impossible to focus, a face I recognised blurred behind it ticking a box in my memory.

"Who was it?"

"I don't know."

"But you saw them, right?"

"Yes. The hotel. The farm."

"What did he look like?"

"The postman. It was his birthday."

"I was afraid of that. My husband."

"My nose is now a feature of my right cheek."

"I'm sorry," she said.

"You haven't done anything."

"I feel responsible."

"You didn't throw the punch."

"I know."

"Your husband?"

"Only legally. Haven't been together for years but he's always had trouble accepting it."

"One way of putting it."

"He's not a bad person. He just feels things strongly."

"I feel it strongly." I smiled and she smiled back. "It's okay," I said, "I'll live."

"I should have told you. I didn't think it was worth it. These things get in the way." There was silence for a while before she spoke again. "Does it hurt very much?"

I thought about my answer. "Does *what* hurt?"

"He was beautiful and he had a personality as big as a mountain. Everyone loved him. I loved him. But I went to London and he couldn't handle it. I realised within days of being there that it was a different world. He wanted me to stay as I was. We should never have got married. My fault. I felt sorry for him and thought it would be okay. I came back but he wouldn't let me be *me*. You wouldn't think it now, but he was beautiful. It's the booze. Are you going to press charges?"

"Hadn't even crossed my mind."

"Are you?"

"Why would I?"

"Just thought you would."

I shook my head. "I don't see what that would achieve."

She looked into her lap, turned her hands over, looked at her nails.

"Are you all right?" I prompted.

"What are we doing?"

"Doing?"

"I haven't met anyone like you before."

"What's that supposed to mean?"

"I don't know."

There was my skull with light shining through it.

"Fine. No fractures," the doctor said. "You've got concussion though, so we'll keep you in."

"I don't want to stay in."

"You haven't got a choice. We need to fix that nose and keep an eye on you. You've had a bang."

"My head's banging."

"Not surprised." He held my head in his hands and looked at me. "Looks as if you'll have *circumorbital ecchymosis* to be proud of, too. That's a shiner to you. Maybe two."

"He couldn't deal with the skulls and bones, either. Said I was weird. Called me a witch one day. Makes sense because he never went away. Poor thing's known nothing but this place. If you don't get out of it your mind remains enclosed by the hills. No, not enclosed, closed. It's a wonderful place but you've got to leave it to know it."

"You didn't know it?"

"No. Couldn't wait to leave. Hated it. But the world is here. I go to London a few times a year for a fix. Take in one of the galleries or an exhibition and it'll nourish me until I feel the need to go again."

"Let me," she said, turning my head to the left and the right with her hand under my chin. She viewed my head from all angles. "It's good. They've done a good job. Now, if you're ready to go, there's something I want you to see."

Chapter Twenty-Five

"This is my studio," she said. The padlock snapped open as she turned the key. The open door revealed a shed about twelve feet by ten. I stepped inside. Everything had been painted white.

"I love it," I said.

"Dad put the see-through roof on. It's just right for me. I don't work on a grand scale."

There was a window along one wall in front of which was a bench. There was a piece of work on it which I picked up. "You work in stone."

"Not just, but often."

"This feels good," I said, passing it from one hand to the other.

"It's from the river. I love what the river does to a stone."

"It's really lovely. Wish I knew how to talk about it."

"But you like it."

"Yes."

"Good. Why should you be able to talk about it? Your education's history not art."

"It was nearly German!"

Shelves displayed more work and a variety of objects. Skulls and bones. She saw me looking.

"That's what I find when I'm out and about. I bring them back if I like them."

"Something to work from."

"I hope they'll move something inside me but I don't pressure myself to come up with something. It doesn't work to force it. My head's in my hands. I express myself with them. I love it when I have something in them and I'm trying to make something else, something new. They help me to understand what's around me."

"Like when I make a model."

"I don't think so."

"But I am trying to understand something."

"I'm manipulating and exploring."

"I'm exploring."

"You're not getting to your father if that's what you mean."

"I think I am."

"A bit of plastic isn't going to help."

"You're being self-righteous. Why should what you do be any better than making a model?"

"That's not true. I'm not. It's…you can't compare them."

"You *are* comparing. You're denigrating the models and why I make them."

"I'm not. I just mean that you can't equate one with the other."

"That's right. You should've said that."

"I'm sorry. I didn't mean to be so strong. Look, I *see* something, I *feel* something, and then I try and understand and interpret it by making it two or three dimensional. It's not model-making."

"I don't think I'm making models. I think I'm looking into the world my father knew. I imagine the physical world around him. I know some of it. I try to fill in gaps with the models."

"*This* is my world. *This* is the place I need."

"This shed?"

She laughed. "I call it my studio, but yes, this shed. And this area."

"Doesn't compare to London."

"I only went there to study. I never intended staying. I was always coming back. I've always felt as if I'm cupped in someone's hands here. These hills. I've never felt it anywhere else. And I can walk into them and know I'll always be fine. This place is in my blood and my bones. It feeds everything within me. Well, nearly."

"Nearly?"

"Yes, nearly." She looked at me intensely. "You don't know what I'm saying, do you?"

"No."

She bit her top lip and scrunched her eyes at me.

"I'm sorry?"

"It's nothing."

I haven't *looked* at a naked woman for years. Of course I can't get away from those I see in the course of my everyday life, in magazines and films and newspapers, but I haven't seen a naked woman in the flesh, next to me, with me, a woman I know I shall touch. When we make love I'm not looking at her as I'm looking at her now. She stands in front of the mirror and is brushing through her hair so that the line of her neck extends and I am aware of the line of her spine defined by the shadows thrown by the shoulder blades, each vertebra a station on the way to her head. The muscles in her back are defined by the particular play of light in the room. Then I look at her in the mirror. She notices me looking.

"Good morning," she says.

"You're beautiful."

She smiles and continues with her hair. Because of the way she is standing, her breasts and stomach are lifted. She turns to face me. She sees me looking and looks down herself.

"I do my bikini line."

"It's your neck I love."

"Neck?" she laughs. "You're a daft thing, aren't you?" She kneels onto the bed and makes her way to my side. "My neck?" she says, running her fingers from her chin down to that niche where it slots into her chest. I kiss it as lightly as I can, then lick it, then bite it, gently. She grips my penis. "Isn't it amazing," she said, "that there's no bone in it?"

I just made a sound which meant agreement.

"Seems to have a joint, too."

She held my hard penis in her hand and moved it back and forth then side to side. She held it between her hands as if they were the two halves of a hot dog. I was aware that I'd had this thought when I was growing up.

"I was nervous about showing you my studio," she said.

"What was there to be nervous about?"

"It was like showing you around inside my head."

I stroked her hair. "It's a lovely head," I said. "It's mine that's broken."

Chapter Twenty-Six

My father sits in a field of wheat and lights a cigarette. His Fort is ablaze nearby and a farmer levels his shotgun at him. My father proffers a cigarette. Then he reaches to a pocket and the farmer shouts *Nein!* Father smiles and moves very slowly and produces a photograph: *Das is ein foto von meinem sohn.* He smiles as he offers the photograph in his outstretched hand.

"Sir! Sir! Are you all right?" There's a man with a medal on his chest shaking me. "You ok? You're making a lot of noise." It's not a medal, it's a name tag. The train guard. "Are you all right, Sir? You look as if you've been in the wars."

"I'm fine thanks, really. Looks worse than it is. It's getting better."

"You sure? Can I get you a coffee or something?"

"No, it's fine." He nodded and went down the carriage towards the front of the train and looked back at me as he went through the door.

"I see you went in the wrong pub," George said.

"Not quite. Her husband. Was her husband."

"I hope you managed to get one in yourself."

"I didn't know what hit me."

"Shame."

"I think I've hurt him."

"Stealing women has never been an endearing quality," he said, smiling.

"It was much worse than this," I said, pointing to my face. "Nose had to be reset."

"I suppose that's the welcome in the hillsides," he said dryly.

"I'm not going to stay at the hotel next time. I'm going to stay with her."

"That's good. What about her husband?"

"I think he's got me out of his system now."

"I hope so. You don't want to reset your nose after each encounter."

The sun was low and cold, the fields' large flats of water undisturbed and as bright as mercury. Half a dozen swans were doubled. The only cloud gauzed the sun's dulled colours, threw the doors and windows of farms into relief. Snow on sheep, cows around a feeding frame. The trees like finely wrought jewellery. Buzzards hunched on branches. Crows flurried across a field. I wondered if the architect of a church considered the clumping of snow on its ledges in its design. Ponies necked and rubbed. Streams ran clear through it all.

The train emerged from the Severn Tunnel to a dying light. Soon the train passed the huge Llanwern works whose low blue sheds never seemed to end. Newport was like steel on this late November afternoon. I went into the café to escape the grey sky and the feeling of claustrophobia the overhanging building caused. I was aware that trains were coming and going when I looked out of the café window at a train trundling past slowly and heavily. My train.

I had been somewhere. Dead ground. History was full of such spaces, gaps between events. People came into the café and trains were announced and the people left. They knew where they were going. There were no gaps for them. The world darkened on the platform. Streetlights lit overhanging buildings in lurid yellow light.

There was a space within me which felt as if it was waiting.

I needed to get on the train. I needed to get the next one. By the time it arrived I knew I'd be travelling through darkness.

Lights suspended from lampposts indicated the proximity of Christmas. Rows of streetlights dotted up hills that headlights plunged down. Kitchens lit up behind curtains, glimpses of TVs, conservatories, lamps on tables. And in the gaps in between, me, in a striped pullover, not wanting to look at myself, and the table in front of me on which I'd placed my ticket for inspection.

The lights outside seemed to go on too long and I worried that I had boarded the wrong train. I had watched my train go out once and now I was going to the wrong place. The lights stopped. I was in a tube going forwards through the darkness. *Dad, are you there? You went through the darkness through lights that were trying to knock you down.* Lights outside again. A station. Yellow light. A stop on the way.

No one gets off and no one gets on. The next station. Ten minutes or thereabouts. I mustn't miss it. I concentrate on not disappearing, on not going to the place which is empty. I'm nearly there. I see the outlines of the hills hunched in the cold night air. The taxi-driver's face is lit by the glow from the dashboard. Bridge Street, Crickhowell. Please.

Chapter Twenty-Seven

I heard her coming down the stairs before she appeared. She had something behind her back.

"What's this?" she said, revealing my dressing gown.

"What's it look like?"

"Well, I know what it *is* but tell me it's not yours."

"It's mine."

"I bet you wear pyjamas too."

"I put them under the pillow."

"Bloody hell!"

"What's wrong with a dressing gown and pyjamas?"

"I've got nothing against either but, one, why do you *wear* pyjamas and two, who ever took a dressing gown anywhere?"

"Can't see the problem myself."

"Obviously. You *are* an old fogey, aren't you?"

Something hurt then. It wasn't her, but something about myself, something related to who I had become.

"I'm sorry. You're bruised," she said, after her last words had silenced me.

"It's okay. You need to say these things. I've been in a little world, I think."

"I'm sorry."

"It's okay, really. I don't want you to stop telling me what you think."

I am stroking the map of her back. I can see the escarpment beneath each shoulder blade, the contours around each buttock, trig points I mark with a kiss. Then there's the valley between them where I like to run my tongue. Sitting on her thighs, I put my hands either side of her waist, gently move them up the ribs and over her shoulders, push my fingers hard into either side of her spine from where her head and neck join, down to the buttocks again. Exposing the vertebra like this makes me aware of each segment. I walk my fingers up the spine as if it's a ridge. She makes noises of pleasure, nuzzles her face further into her folded arm.

I kiss places on her back. "This is a cairn, this is a pile of stones, this is a reservoir." Then I trace the outline of a shoulder blade with my tongue from the inside to the soft skin beneath her arm. "This is a mountain stream."

"That tickles," she squirms. She turns over so that I am sitting on her lap. She looks at me. "What about you?" She strokes me below the navel.

"The contour lines would be close together there," I say.

"It's real," she says.

"I'm embarrassed by it."

"Well I don't want you to change it. It's an honest tummy."

"Honest! I've never thought of it as that."

"It's a landscape I like."

I laughed. "Good. I hope you enjoy the views."

"What's stopping you from going up the hill?"

"I don't know."

"You've come all this way and you can't walk up a hill."

"I don't *know* what it is. I think after all these years I'm not ready. I mean, I'm ready, but I'm not prepared."

"I don't know what you have to be prepared *for*."

That knocked me. There was something within me which lifted then. She was right. I was going up an empty hill. There would be nothing to see but other hills. Everything I was doing was a way for me to get to know him in some way, to understand him. "You're right," I said.

"So what's stopping you?"

"Nothing. Nothing now. Thank you."

"For?"

"Just thank you."

I had already stood in the hedge for the milk lorry to pass, and a Landrover. Then the post van came. The sun flashed off the windscreen and the sun-blind was down, so I couldn't see the driver. It came at speed, swerving at the kinks where the lane accommodated the contours of the hill. I stepped into the side where the mud was pushed by tractors and the van came on. It hit the bank and came at me. There was nowhere to go. I ran across the lane and jumped at the fence exposed on that side, catching myself on the top strand of barbed wire.

When I picked myself up I was slicked with mud and my trousers were ripped, exposing my thigh, bleeding.

I was in the shower when she came into the bathroom.

"Well, what was it like?"

"I didn't get there."

"Oh, not again. I'm going to shoot you."

"I fell."

"That's just an excuse. You know that."

"Scratched my leg getting over a fence."

"I'm beginning to worry about you. Doesn't look good, does it, not being able to get over a fence? Perhaps I should go with you, make sure you get there, keep you out of trouble."

"It was just one of those things." I stepped out of the shower and she saw the cut, open and deep.

"For goodness' sake, that's not a scratch!"

"It's fine."

"It needs stitches."

"That's what they said in the pharmacy when I called in for sticking plaster."

"They're right."

"Butterflies are fine. It's what my mother did when I was a boy."

"It's ragged."

"It's clean. You don't go to hospital for a scratch."

"It looks sore."

"It is, but it's fine. Really."

"You're a dull sod."

"Thanks."

"It's good. I love it. It's one of the things I love about you. You're not on the make. You're not out to impress. You're just, just..."

"Don't sound very interesting to me."

"Oh you are, you *are*."

"The more you say the less I like it."

"You're *hope*less."

"Please, no more."

"I love it. You're taking it all wrong. Everything I'm saying is good. It's wonderful. I love you, for God's sake."

I found myself looking at the floor. She told me that she loved me and I looked at the floor. A woman. She. She told me. I had looked at her and imagined sex with her and now she said she loved me. I didn't think about this. I had wanted to feel her skin against mine, that soft glide of warmth as our stomachs touched. She loved me. She said.

"I don't *know* what love is," I said. I looked at her then. She bit her lip. Her face held on and on and on then unmade. I pulled her to me and she sobbed into my chest. I stroked and kissed her head.

My leg wasn't just hurting because of the cut I had sustained, it was because I had spent my working life walking on the flat and now the hills were pulling in my thighs and calf muscles for the first time. My father in my muscles.

Chapter Twenty-Eight

"A student nicked it from St. Mary's medical school. That was the story, anyway. I loved it, the skeleton, I mean, not the story. It's real, too, not a synthetic one. They used to get them from India, apparently."

"Must have taken a long time."

"Shame I didn't finish it."

"It's fabulous."

It was a large drawing made up of two sheets of paper taped together, folded at the join. It ended at the knuckles of the femurs. It looked left to right as if she had asked it to face that way, yet it was entirely linear with no indication of light and shade. The rest of the skeleton was straight-on. It was a portrait of a personal history, the evidence of life: the set of the jaw, the breadth of the shoulders, the expanse of the chest, the hands' particular finesse that could discriminate between what was hard and soft, strong or weak. The lines did not have the definiteness I would have expected but were light and precise. It was as if they were hinting at what would have been attached to the bones. The shoulders. The pelvis. The eyes. It was suspended from the skull, gibbet-like.

"I concentrated on the spaces," she said. "The tutor was stressing the significance of the spaces. They were as much part of the drawing as the marks we made, and so it was with my sculpture."

"I love it."

"It was only an exercise."

"Can I buy it?"

"Don't be daft."

"Please."

"You can have it if you *really* like it."

"Really?"

"Really. You can have it."

She was wearing a woollen skirt to the top of her knees and black boots with tights. I could *see* her legs even when she was dressed like this. I tried to see her skeleton but I couldn't get past the warmth of her skin, the weight of a leg in my hand, the shape of the calf in my palm, the tiny prick of the hairs as they came through before she shaved again, the alabaster smoothness after shaving.

We left the road and the lane went up around a spur. The trees were dense on the right and the land open to the left. The road levelled off into trees so that there was this strange feeling that I was moving through a canopy of branches and leaves. Stone pillars marked the entrance. The lane gave way to a neat drive to the left of which were lawns and an ornamental pond. The hotel looked Italianate but for its local sandstone. The towers bestowed a kind of gravitas. It was a mile from the main road but felt other-worldly.

The other-worldliness was no less strong inside. It was grand in an understated way. The spaces were large and warm. There were rods on the walls in the bar, as well as antique maps of Wales and photographs of guests holding up fish they had caught. The same man appeared in several of them. It was the man I had watched catch the trout.

"I met *him* on the river," I said, indicating the man in a photograph standing with a woman holding a salmon.

"Really? Then I won't have to introduce you when you meet. That's *my* father. He's a guide here."

We sat down to coffee. White cups. Cafétière. Biscuits. Then she took my hand and led me outside onto the terrace and the wall. "This is my idea of heaven," she said.

From the terrace there was an emptiness that stepped away from the hotel and its towers. The sound of the river where it tumbled over stones came up to us. The oak on the bank there looked like a huge lung. The specimen trees to our left formed a symmetry with the towers. Apart from the fir copse on top of the hill opposite, the trees along the river and the hedges were large and separate. Small birds – tits and finches – moved in them. The grass was the green-yellow of winter, the ferns rust patches of flattened bracken. It *was* beautiful, but heaven? I smiled at her.

"Bats fly all around here in the summer." She took my hand again and we went down some steps. "They fly in and out of here," she said, pointing along a row of arches.

The bat was on the bench in the second arch, a brittle folded leaf. "Poor thing," she said. She examined it closely. "It's so fine." Her eyes filled with tears. She put it into my hands gently. Its wings were folded around itself like a tattered shroud.

"Let's put it somewhere safe."

We went back up the steps to the car and lay it on the back seat. Then we walked into the garden. An old acer on the lawn was a contortion of knuckles and leaf litter. The massive gunnera next to the pond looked like a theatrical spider that had collapsed. The clock tower's faces told the wrong time. Moles had broken up the lawn near the steps we took down to the path to the river. The water level was higher than the summer so that there were fewer stones exposed, and the tall grasses and reeds that were mid-stream features were absent. The water was the astonishing clarity that snow-melt and a crisp day create. Where was life? Where were the trout now? There was no sound at all when we stopped to look at something. It was like the silence of a cold church. Then the sounds the river made could be discerned, the water moving to accommodate the shape of the bed or the way the banks pinched in. A tractor and dog running around it were so distant that their sounds did not register above the river's. A jay came out of the brush in front of us and its white rump and blue wing flashes were intense as it crossed to the other side of the valley.

"This is what I love about winter," she said. "You can see the structure of everything." She was looking at the snowed trees on the opposite bank. "Look at those. Beautiful skeletons. Branches begetting branches, smaller and smaller, filling the space, the air. That's what good sculpture does. It suggests another life, another season, if you like."

"Do you see sculpture in everything?"

"More or less."

"Really?"

"It's how I see *all* people. I see the structures supporting them."

"The physical ones."

"The physical ones can indicate other structures, but it's the scaffold I'm interested in." She took off her gloves and pulled the glove off my right hand. She felt each finger separately, from the knuckle to the tip, pressed the space between the forefinger and thumb. "You have good hands," she said. "They're well made. You could do something with these."

"Like what?"

She unbuttoned her jacket and slipped my hand under her pullover to touch her belly.

"You'll get cold," I said.

She moved my hand up to her breast and clasped it there. "Feel what's underneath," she said. She looked at me hard and I looked along my arm to where my hand went under her pullover. "What do you feel?"

"Warmth."

"What else?"

"Bone."

"Concentrate." She gripped my wrist. "Feel," she said, "*feel.*"

"The edge of your bra."

"You've lost it," she said. "What's beneath, what's be*neath.*" She took my hand away.

"I'm sorry. Perhaps it's because my hands are cold."

"Maybe."

"What do you want me to feel?"

"You'll know when you feel it."

"Spaces?"

"You'll *know.*"

Back at the car she tapped the back window. "We need to find a place for him," she said, indicating the bat.

She got in and opened the passenger door for me. "What makes you think it's a he?"

"Something about him. Why, do you think he's a she?"

"No."

"Well, then."

"Okay, he's a *he*."

I looked at that part of her leg between the bottom of her skirt and the top of her boot and put my hand on it. Her muscles moved as she depressed the clutch. She looked at me and smiled. "I love your thighs," I said. I squeezed. I ran my hand over her knee then.

"I've got to drive."

She drove slowly and only accelerated when clear of the gates. Pine needles. Leaf litter. The trunks of the trees either side of us were spindly yet the more I looked into them the more dense they became. I took out my compass and held it in my lap.

"What've you got that for?"

"I like to watch the needle as we change direction."

"It doesn't change direction."

"That's what I mean."

"Well, you don't need to worry, I know where we're going."

The needle kept indicating north as everything moved around it. We turned onto the main road and didn't get far before we were stopped by a police car across the road. She wound down her window.

"Where you going?"

"Just to Crick."

"Sorry, Love, can't let you through. There's been an accident. You'll have to turn round and go in another way."

"Hope they're okay," she said, as she turned the car around.

She dropped me in the High Street outside the grocer's.

"See you at the house," she said.

In the moment when the lock cleared the receiver I knew something was wrong. The air had been disturbed. Something crunched underfoot. The room looked as if a tornado had visited. The lamp was snapped, table upturned, shelves and skulls smashed to smithereens. There was blood on the walls. I ran around looking for her. A force had flailed in the space and cut itself so that its blood had smeared the walls. But I thought that it was her blood, that *she'd* been disassembled. There was a space within me shaped like her. I thought I'd find her in pieces in the kitchen. No. Perhaps she'd been broken in her bedroom or bathroom. No. The space within hurt.

The kitchen was untouched. I ran up the stairs. The spare room, the bedroom, the bathroom. All intact. A shout from downstairs then: "What the fuck! What the fuck!"

I hurt my ankle taking the stairs two at a time. She stood in the bones with the bat in her hands. The space within me filled as if water rushed in.

"Why did he do this? Why?"

I put my arms around her and pulled her tight into my chest. She cried. "There's blood on the walls," I said. "I thought it was you."

"Why why why why why?"

"I don't know."

"Why would he do this to me?"

"I thought you were hurt."

"I *am* hurt!"

"I thought he'd killed you."

"I'm gonna fucking kill *him*!"

I held her until she calmed down. I relaxed my arms and we sat on the floor amidst the debris. "We'll clean up, come on."

"My things. All my things."

"Look," I said. I placed the bat on the mantelpiece. "We can start again."

"Why would he do this?"

"I don't know."

"It's you."

"I'm sorry."

"He can't deal with you."

"What are you going to do?"

"Kill him."

"He might hurt you."

"No, he won't hurt me. He'd never hurt me. Not physically, anyway. He just makes lots of noise and breaks things." A car door clunked outside.

Then there was a knock. I opened the door. It was her father. Then two police officers appeared, one male, one female.

"Head-on," the female officer said.

"He died at the scene," the male officer added.

"I said I was going to kill him."

The officers looked at each other, looked at me. I explained.

She sat looking into space. Then she put the bat in my hands. "I can't have him here. Find him somewhere else."

"We'll leave you alone for now," the female officer said. "We'll be in touch."

Her father stood up and put his arms around her. "Can you give us some time?"

3.30pm in early December. Stillness in St. Peter's. I stood with my back against the heavy oak door I'd just closed, the light from the west window lighting a patch of ceiling with its distorted shape. This side of the church, with its four windows showing the story of the Good Samaritan, was lit by a high glow. The north side of the building, separated by six arches, felt as if it was in a kind of sleep. Here there was a red carpet between the pews that led to the altar. Clear glass framed three stained glass figures in the window above it: Christ in majesty flanked by St. Peter holding keys and St. Paul holding jointed wood. A candle in a red glass burned low in the dish suspended from the beam above.

I stepped over the rope and stood at the cloth-draped altar. I placed the bat carefully as if I were putting it down to sleep. It looked like a swaddled child. It looked good on the white cloth.

The sound of the latch dropping echoed through the church.

The very tip of the sun slipped behind the horizon and lit the sky white immediately along that part of the ridge. A jet scratched along the blue over Crug Hywel. Snow and ice crunched on the path to the lychgate through which I had entered the churchyard.

Chapter Twenty-Nine

The lane became a track more suited to four wheel drives so that I had to manoeuvre this way and that in order not to catch the bottom of the car on jutting stones, or end up in a ditch. After about a mile I parked the car where the track ran out and a gate blocked the way ahead. I put the bag on my back and set off, map in hand. The trees darkened the way ahead, their trunks tall and warm where the sun pierced the canopy. A stream spilled alongside the track until disappearing and emerging noisily the other side to another stream running down the valley.

I aimed for a bend in the track where I emerged from one clump of trees and before I met the next. There was a stile in the fence and a path the other side which took a diagonal route up the side of the open hill, my boots' treads like tyre marks in the earth.

Moving up a hill – one of *these* hills, one which moves into the line of another and supports it – was new to me. It's done in stages. It's not something you just *do*. It's a process – though process makes it sound mechanical when in fact it's emotional. You put your *self* into it, you move in a scene. It's like taking on a different state, something beyond what you are.

The top of the hill is a long way off and you move towards it gradually, doing stretches, setting yourself a little goal each time – that clump, that bend in the path, that pile of stones – and when you reach each one you stop and take in your new perspective – seeing things you couldn't see the last time you stopped – and you feel the sweat on your back, the pull in your calf, the need to take water. In this way I got to know something about where I was.

The first I saw of him was as something very small moving on the skyline. This became a head, then head and shoulders and so on until his whole figure came into view, moving casually along the top of the hill as I approached from below. I stopped to take in what was around me and when I started again he was on the top. He had a thick stick and it was some time before I realised that it was a rolled umbrella. As I got closer his appearance took me by surprise: jacket and tie, pressed trousers, gleaming shoes. His hair was as white as cloud. He looked at me for longer than I expected, then raised his umbrella to me. I waved. He nodded, then turned and walked away.

I had been too busy watching the next step to have seen what he had been doing at the top. He was on his way when I looked at the route on the map which had brought me to this point, taking in the hills around me, the forestry, tracks and lanes. From here the map shows the way to Grwyne Fawr Reservoir and I look around three hundred and sixty degrees. There: Pen Twyn Mawr; there: Hatterrall Hill; there: Crug Hywel; there: Pen Twyn Glas. The man with the umbrella was distant now, his white hair bright against the greens and browns of the hill. Then I found it. A cairn of nine stones. That was all. I looked around. Nine. I found a stone of a good size and weight and placed it on the top. I had come all this way to find a missing stone.

I sat on the damp earth and took the crumpled envelope from my bag and opened it:

I wonder when you will read this? Will you be seven, eight, nine years old? Your mother will know best. I am sure that whenever you read it, you will be a fine man.

It is sad for me to write this because it means that we shall never have known each other. Well, I have known you in one sense, held you in my arms where you have slept. We have fallen asleep together in a chair in your grandparents' home. But we shall not have known each other to talk and share what there is in this life to share. And now I find I must apologise for that because you might not yet understand what it is I am referring to. One day.

There are a few things I would have loved to have shared with you. First, I would have liked to have flown with you by my side. Second, I would have liked to have taught you how to fish. Third, I wanted to tell you about Marty, the best friend I ever had who could find a single trout in a stretch of river where no one else could. There were times when I thought that to be able to find them he must have been a trout in a former life!

I wonder, too, when you reach my age – I am twenty-two years old now – what you will be doing? I trust the world won't be as crazy as the one in which I am writing this, in which people do terrible things to each other. We must all get along. We must try. It's important for you to understand that the world doesn't have to be like this.

I expect your mother will teach you the flowers of the fields as she taught me, and that your grandfather will teach you country ways. Perhaps you will go to St. Michael's church where your mother and I were married. There is a tomb there to the Fitzroy family on which Noah's Ark is part of the frieze. It's wonderful. It reminds me of my aeroplane because we call our aeroplanes ships, and the sea looks like clouds. I run my hands over it each time I visit. Touch it, then you will know that our bodies have received the same knowledge from the same thing in the same place. The thought of you doing so comforts me now.

If I were there to guide you, advise you, I would say that each person has a place. You will find it in your own time. It will be a moment when your life makes sense. It will happen, I promise you. My place is not with you from now on. Something has determined that I have lived my time. I'm done.

Look after your mother. She's the best.

With you always,

Dad x

A raven *kraanked* above me and floated in the big sky. The man with the white hair was distant. He stopped, turned to face me, held out his arms like wings for a long, long, long, long, long time. Then he fell to the ground.

EPILOGUE

Body Mystery

Police are trying to identify the body of a man found by a walker near Crickhowell last Sunday.
"The man was carrying no means of identification," Inspector Gareth John of Dyfed and Powys Police told The Chronicle.

The man, believed to be in his seventies, was wearing a blue blazer, white shirt and red tie. "It's a mystery," Inspector John added. "He was not dressed for walking on the hills but was carrying an umbrella."

He is described as having white hair and being approximately 6'4" tall.

A post-mortem failed to establish the cause of death.

"Someone must know this man. If anyone has any information which could help us identify this person, please come forward and help solve this mystery," added Inspector John.

Behind the door were fifty empty years.

"Problem with the lock?" she said.

"No, no." The door swung open over a pile of mail. I stepped aside. "*My* Hovis house."

"Thank you," she smiled, going in front of me. She stood in the hall and looked around, then went into the sitting room while I picked up the mail and went through to the kitchen with the bread and milk we'd picked up on the way. She was talking to herself but I couldn't make out what she was saying. The sounds were pleasing. There was a woman in my house, a different woman.

"Cosy," she said, appearing in the kitchen doorway.

"It's all I've known."

"I like it."

"Bit old fashioned?"

"And male. To be expected, I suppose."

"Go and have a look out there," I said, unlocking the back door for her.

In a while she called, "Plenty of room for a workshop!"

"You could have a big one." I stood at the back door shielding my eyes from the sun. "Coffee's ready!"

She took the mug and looked at me over the rim when she sipped. She picked up the car keys from the table. "I'll bring my stuff in."

I was looking out of the kitchen window at the garden when she called me into the sitting room. There was the raven's skull next to my father on the mantelpiece. "I didn't know you'd repaired it."

"Glue, patience and time, that's all."

"Time is ours, now," I said.

Granddad drummed it into me: never close the gun by lifting the barrels to the stock, but lift the stock and keep the barrels pointing at the ground; break the gun and empty it when you negotiate an obstacle; make sure it's empty and pass it to a fellow shooter so that they can *see* that the chambers are empty; never load the gun indoors. So if he'd seen me drop a cartridge into the barrel and close the gun in my bedroom, he would have hit me from here to next week.

I beaded the Fortress suspended from the ceiling and pulled the trigger. The shot boomed in the enclosed space and the Fortress went all over the room. Obliterated.

The dust was falling on me when she rushed into the room.

~

CPSIA information can be obtained at www.ICGtesting.com
Printed in the USA
LVOW06s1504300314

379543LV00003B/359/P

About the Author

JEREMY HUGHES was born in Crickhowell, south Wales. He was awarded first prize in the Poetry Wales competition and his poetry was short-listed for an Eric Gregory Award. He has published two pamphlets - *breathing for all my birds* (2000) and *The Woman Opposite* (2004) - and has published poetry, short fiction, memoir and reviews widely in British and American magazines. He studied for the Master's in Creative Writing at the University of Oxford. His first novel *Dovetail* was published in 2011.

Acknowledgements

There is a leaflet published by the Brecon Beacons National Park titled "Aircraft crash sites and the stories behind them". Of the thirty crash sites described, number twenty-three recounts the fate of Flying Fortress 42-5903 "Ascend Charlie" which crashed 16th September 1943. The ten crew members were killed. This book is also dedicated to them.

I would like to thank Susan Trolley and family for their generous hospitality, and John Ballam for his friendship and advice.